BOA
EDITIONS LTD

WHERE CAN I TAKE YOU
WHEN THERE'S NOWHERE TO GO

WHERE CAN I TAKE YOU WHEN THERE'S NOWHERE TO GO

Stories

JOE BAUMANN

AMERICAN READER SERIES, NO. 40

BOA EDITIONS, LTD. ‡ ROCHESTER, NY ‡ 2023

First Edition
23 24 25 26 7 6 5 4 3 2 1

For information about permission to reuse any material from this book, please contact The Permissions Company at www.permissionscompany.com or e-mail permdude@ gmail.com.

Publications by BOA Editions, Ltd.—a not-for-profit corporation under section 501 (c) (3) of the United States Internal Revenue Code—are made possible with funds from a variety of sources, including public funds from the Literature Program of the National Endowment for the Arts; the New York State Council on the Arts, a state agency; and the County of Monroe, NY. Private funding sources include the Max and Marian Farash Charitable Foundation; the Mary S. Mulligan Charitable Trust; the Rochester Area Community Foundation; the Ames-Amzalak Memorial Trust in memory of Henry Ames, Semon Amzalak, and Dan Amzalak; the LGBT Fund of Greater Rochester; and contributions from many individuals nationwide. See Colophon on page 208 for special individual acknowledgments.

Cover Design: Daphne Morrissey
Interior Design and Composition: Isabella Madeira
BOA Logo: Mirko

BOA Editions books are available electronically through BookShare, an online distributor offering Large-Print, Braille, Multimedia Audio Book, and Dyslexic formats, as well as through e-readers that feature text to speech capabilities.

Cataloging-in-Publication Data is available from the Library of Congress.

BOA Editions, Ltd.
250 North Goodman Street, Suite 306
Rochester, NY 14607
www.boaeditions.org
A. Poulin, Jr., Founder (1938-1996)

For anyone who thinks there's nowhere to go

CONTENTS

‡

We Adore These Bodies Until They Are Gone	9
Clinging	25
Hollowed Grounds	39
Forgotten Folk	53
Heave Your Dead to the Ground	71
For Rent	83
I Will Eat You, Drink You, I Will Be Full	95
Look at Me	111
Boys With Faces Like Mirrors	125
Happy Birthdays	135
Where Can I Take You When There's Nowhere To Go	139
You Cannot Contain What's Built Up Inside	159
A Million Hearts Can't All Be Broken	173
Upon a Cutting	187
Acknowledgments	*203*
About the Author	*204*
Colophon	*208*

WE ADORE THESE BODIES UNTIL
THEY ARE GONE

Eddie and I had been going to Padilla's for eight weeks when
we saw an evaporation.

We'd discovered the bar, which had previously been a state
auction house, and before that a barn, on the outskirts of Thomasville, a few weeks after we moved. We were desperate for a
place to become regulars after it became clear that Eddie's new
colleagues in the English department were mostly homebodies
who actively despised one another and had simply put on a good
show during Eddie's campus visit. One of his students mentioned
Padilla's in passing and so we checked it out. The poolhall had
absurdly high ceilings—you could see the traces of the hayloft
and horse stalls—but good lighting. Two bartenders worked two
bars, one for beer drinkers and the other for those interested in
the harder stuff. If you wanted wine, you stayed in town.

The parking lot was across the two-lane state highway that
ribboned off to the west of Thomasville, but hardly any cars passed
by on Friday nights, so crossing was never a problem. On the night
of the evaporation, Eddie and I were wearing nearly-matching
jeans and sweaters thanks to the fall chill; his green was a shade
lighter than mine. If the clientele—mostly grumbling men who
worked at the various mechanics shops and the farm supply store
in town—had any idea that we were a couple, they didn't show it.
We ordered our beers and found a booth; they lined every wall,
interrupted only by the two bars and the doors to the restrooms.

The only other seating was the barstools, as the center of Padilla's was occupied by its dozen pool tables.

The music was kept low, and it cycled between the country twang of Patsy Cline and Merle Haggard and the heavy hip hop of Wiz Khalifa and Drake, with a smattering of Kansas, Boston, and Journey in between. When the evaporation happened, a Nelly song had just concluded, and right before Willie Nelson started crowing, the sound of shattering glass rang out through the bar, a pint dropped on the concrete floor. At first, people started applauding, but then they stopped, as did Eddie, when they saw the source: right next to the detonated puddle of beer and glass was a heap of clothing: jeans and a checked shirt mounded over a pair of shoes. A watch sat atop the pile like an offering. The bartender, a woman named Lake who had snaky tattoos inking their way up each arm, stared at the empty space in front of her where, seconds before, a man had stood. Now, the only thing there was the slightest vapory haze that every single person in Padilla's watched dissipate into nothing.

‡

I first saw an evaporation when I was fifteen. The only athletic thing I was any good at was swimming, so I'd joined my high school team even though I'd at first been terrified of wearing a Speedo; I was tall and skinny and my hipbones flared like elephant ears. In the months before my first practice, I spent every morning doing pushups and crunches and squats next to my bed, and my body was always aching. But I saw growth, slowly, and even though I knew I'd still be stick-skinny next to the other boys, I felt stronger and bigger. It was something.

Danny Beakerman was a junior and one of our fastest freestylers. His cheeks were ruddy as if he was always recovering from being backhanded, and his blaze of red hair reminded me of autumn. Danny was popular, and his letterman jacket looked good on him. He usually swam in the lane next to mine and always complimented my form and my improved times. Danny was constantly smiling. But then, during a practice in early spring of my sophomore year, we were swimming two hundreds. Danny had been ahead of me by a length or two, taking it easy, and then suddenly he wasn't there. Through the splashing of other swimmers I could hear our coach's whistle, so when I reached the wall, I stopped, popping up to the surface. I tossed off my goggles to see what was going on. My ears were plugged with water, my nose with chlorine. I saw Danny's Speedo, deep black against the aquamarine of the water. I felt my stomach roll. I looked around. Half of my teammates clung to the lane lines, as if they were lost at sea. Because I was closest to the spot where Danny evaporated, I felt as if all eyes were on me. Of course, no one was actually paying any attention to me.

Staring through the water, I tried to see some trace of Danny Beakerman, but the only evidence he'd been in the pool was his abandoned Speedo floating up to the chopped surface. His vaporized self was seething through the chlorine and water, and I imagined all those invisible molecules bobbing in my direction. I sunk down just so, letting the stinging liquid lap into my open mouth. Perhaps I was retaining the last pieces of Danny before they became nothing. I tried to taste them flowing between my lips, but all I could sense was the harsh chemicals. Whatever Danny had been was gone.

‡

No one wanted to touch the evaporated man's clothes. Lake stared at them and eventually she swept up the broken glass with a broom and dustpan, her movements shaky but careful; she skittered around his discarded jeans like they were infectious. That wasn't how the evaporations worked, but fear is a powerful intoxicant, as strong as the cheap tequila and whiskey behind the bar.

Eddie drank his beer and went up to order us two more. I stared toward the heap of clothes. I knew nothing about the man, but a bar seemed like an incongruous place to evaporate. I wondered if the people he'd arrived with had any clue that he might want to vanish from the world. Then I wondered if he'd arrived with anyone. None of the other drinkers at the bar seemed overly stunned by the man's evaporating, and after the initial shock wore off, everyone went on drinking their beers or floating over to a pool table as if nothing had happened.

When Eddie slid back into the booth, setting a bottle of Amberbock in front of me, he let out a long, hissing exhalation. "You okay?" he said.

"Why wouldn't I be?"

"It's a strange thing to see."

"We didn't technically see it. Just the aftermath."

Eddie picked at the label of his beer bottle, peeling it off in wet chunks that he rolled into tight cylinders. I read somewhere once, or was maybe told by an idiot at a party who'd seen me doing the same thing, that this was a sign of sexual frustration. Eddie had been tired lately, the slough of the tenure line getting to him even though he was on a three-three teaching load and not expected to take on committee or advising work in his first year. But he was coming home looking more and more tired every day. He was constantly bringing stacks of student assignments (Eddie was big into "reader response"), leaving them heaped on his desk in the spare bedroom of the house we were renting. They never seemed to go out the door with him in the morning.

"Do you want to go home?" I said finally.

"Why would I want to do that?"

I shrugged toward the heap of abandoned clothes. The longer they sat there, the more absurd the situation seemed. They were just jeans and a shirt.

"You seem upset."

"I do?" Eddie said.

"Distracted."

"Oh." He drank and set the bottle aside. "No. Just thinking of Regan."

I frowned. "Who?"

"My officemate. From two years ago."

"I don't think I ever knew his name."

One of Eddie's officemates in graduate school evaporated right at his desk, hunched over a stack of horrible research papers. When it happened, Eddie said he had no idea that the guy had felt that badly.

"Everyone hates graduate school," he'd said. Then he'd lain on the couch for an entire afternoon, staring up at the ceiling of our apartment. I was worried he would evaporate if I left the room, so I didn't. I muted the television and sat in the rickety recliner we'd bought, the first piece of furniture that belonged to the two of us together. It was a broken thing, barely rocked forward and back, and the leg rest didn't extend all the way, but it had been cheap—we were both poor, Eddie's stipend barely covering his half of the rent and my job at the university bookstore doing us no great financial favors—and it was ours. I sat looking at him, feeling like a therapist, him my patient, but he said nothing. Eventually he roused himself, saying he was hungry. I followed him into the kitchen and we made sandwiches.

Eddie finished his beer and stood to go to the bar, not bothering to ask if I wanted another drink. Padilla's had started to fill up, most of the pool tables taken, the thwack of cue sticks and balls clanging against one another competing with the music, which had shifted to "Don't Stop Me Now." Drinkers hovering nearby were glancing at me, eyeing the booth like primo property; the only free space was that surrounding the evaporated man's clothing, a dead zone that seemed to be growing. I watched as Eddie breached its perimeter to approach the bar. He straddled the pile of clothing, one foot on either side.

Most Fridays, after a trip to Padilla's, Eddie was in the mood for sex, which had become hard to come by since the stress of his job had left him tense and worn. But tonight he was aloof. I could tell he was thinking about the evaporated man, but I couldn't begin to guess what. Or maybe he was thinking about Regan, the officemate; I was certainly thinking about Danny Beakerman. Surely everyone in the bar who had ever seen someone evaporate was thinking of that person.

We laid in the dark for a long time, both of us awake and staring at the ceiling. I tried to speak, but couldn't find words. Every now and then Eddie's lips would move, but no sound came out. Eventually he fell asleep, but I kept staring up at the ceiling, seeing little motes of dust float through the angled beams of moonlight that snuck through the window. I wondered what they were, who they were, if someone who had lived here before us had evaporated and we were surrounded by ghosts, particles carrying muscle and memory across the room forever.

‡

That next Monday, the work request came and I accepted. My undergraduate degree was in art; I'd wanted to be a sculptor when I was a kid. I spent hours imagining my own The Thinker or Christ, the Redeemer. I read about David and the Pieta in books my parents gave me for Christmas. When Eddie got his job, he tried to wrangle a spousal hire even though we weren't married, but because I only had a BFA the best the dean of arts and sciences could offer me was an art appreciation course or two from time to time as an adjunct, which I didn't mind, despite Eddie's bitching about it. The dean also said I could make use of whatever studio facilities I might want.

In my free time, I'd started a business, though that was perhaps a generous description of a crappy Wordpress site through which I accepted orders for miniature sculptures and ceramics. I'd taken a course on mold-making in college, and, in addition to the homemade soaps I made using an immersion blender and an enamelware pot Eddie gave me for my birthday (he thought

I'd start concocting soups during cold weather), I also offered glass and ceramic cast miniature sculptures from a pre-made list I'd created, photographing the wares myself. The site didn't get much traffic, but the orders gave me something to do on the days that I wasn't teaching my one class.

I showed Eddie the order that afternoon.

"They want one hundred dwarves?"

I nodded. My most popular sculpture, for whatever reason, was an eight-inch tall dwarf made of flint clay that I fired and then hand-painted, the hat a ubiquitous red, pants and shirt blue and white, respectively. They didn't take that long, individually, but one hundred was a lot.

"And they want them in two weeks?" he said. "What in the world for?"

I shrugged. "Wedding décor? Table markers or something?"

"Dwarves? At a wedding?"

"I didn't ask," I said.

"Are you going to accept the order?"

"Why not?" I said. "What else am I doing?"

Eddie pursed his lips and nodded. He asked what we should do for dinner. I cooked most nights, but I'd been perplexed by the order and had spent most of the afternoon doing calculations for how much paint and clay I would need, trekking to the one art supply store in town and buying all of their flint. Even so, I'd had to order a bunch online, paying a few extra dollars for expedited shipping. I'd had no time to consider food.

We drove to the town square. Most of Thomasville's economy was reliant on the public university where Eddie taught; its six thousand liberal arts students kept money moving between the dive bars and hole-in-the-wall restaurants and the laundromats. Most of the locally-owned businesses were bunched on a grid near the county courthouse, encircling the building in a fence of one-way streets. We ate at a little Italian place where Eddie had been taken for dinner during his campus visit, each of us ordering an innocuous plate of linguine with marinara sauce. Eddie drank a dark beer that clashed with his food; I stuck to water. The restaurant was almost entirely dead, save for a trio of young men at the small bar near the kitchen; I overheard them order multiple rounds of sambuca.

"Someone's birthday?" I said.

Eddie shrugged, twirling noodles with his fork. "Could be celebrating anything."

"Or mourning," I said.

"Do you think you'll start on your dwarves tomorrow?"

I nodded. "After class." I taught on Tuesday and Thursday mornings. "We could drive together. That way I can't leave until you're ready."

Eddie ate, swallowed, drank from his beer, and then said, "What if you're not ready to leave when I am?"

"I'll always be ready when you're ready."

Eddie rolled his eyes but placed a hand over mine; it was solid, warm. I let him press his fingers down on mine so I knew that neither of us was going anywhere any time soon.

‡

The next morning, as I was gathering my supplies and Eddie was showering, my phone buzzed: an email sent through the site. It was from the woman who had ordered the dwarves. She wanted to know if she could increase her order to 150.

We're having a ceremony, she wrote. *I didn't think so many people would RSVP yes. My wife evaporated. She loved dwarves. She wanted to live in one of those dwarf-houses in South City, you know? Narrow and long with the pitched gables? Is that the right word, gables? I don't know. She collected dwarves. And I saw your dwarf, and I just knew. It would be the perfect way to remember her.*

I didn't tell Eddie about the email. When we parked, he asked if I needed any help carrying my supplies; I shook my head no, even though the bricks of clay were heavy and my arms were throbbing by the time I arrived at the art building. Campus was crammed into a single large square in the middle of town. The buildings were nice, all brick with white concrete trim, names of famous Missourians etched into the archways at the main entrances: the art building was called Benton Hall after the famous muralist, and was home to the art historians, the studio arts, and the theatre department. Final rehearsals for the fall musical were underway, day in and day out, and in the mornings I could hear murmurings of a piano and actors stomping across the stage of the black box theatre. I didn't have time to dump my materials in the studio with the firing kiln, so I took everything with me straight to class.

The students were all non-majors, as the 100-level art appreciation class didn't count toward any of the majors; the thirty-one students were mostly studying business and history, a few English and economics students sprayed around the room. And even though most of them probably had no real interest in the difference between baroque and Fauvism and constructivism, they all pretended well enough. My class was at 9:30, and most of the students were never sleepy or sedate, chattering with one another before I walked in each morning, the noise level only simmering down when I finally cleared my throat and launched into my lecture for that day.

I managed to get through my talk introducing expressionism, clicking through a slideshow of Kirchner, Reiter, Kandinsky and Marc paintings. They jotted down notes, raised their hands with questions, with answers to my inquiries. Then at the end of class, as students were closing their notebooks and zipping up their backpacks, Marshall, a slouchy fraternity boy who always wore a baseball cap pivoted backward and barely took notes but always remembered whatever I'd said the class prior, said, "What's with all the clay, Mr. Davenport?"

I looked down, having managed to briefly forget about the flint stacked next to the podium in its brown bags. "Oh," I said. "It's a project."

"What kind?"

Without thinking about it, I told the class about the order for dwarves. I told them everything, about the woman's email, the memorial. They all stopped packing up, weirdly entranced by the story. Marshall nodded.

"I get it," he said. "My uncle evaporated when I was fifteen. Just about destroyed my mom. He was her only sibling, and my grandparents were already dead."

A girl near the back said, "One of my friends evaporated over the summer. I was at her house. She went into the bathroom and never came out."

They all started talking about their own losses, witnessings, stories they'd heard.

"What about you, Mr. Davenport?" one of them asked.

All eyes slid toward me. I thought about mentioning the man at Padilla's. How the temperature in the bar seemed to spike briefly when the man evaporated, as if all his body heat had spread throughout the room, his kinetic energy finding release in everyone else. How the bar's smells—the felt of the pool tables, the slick spill of beer, the chill autumn air that crept in every time the door opened—had cranked up a notch. The desperate moment of silence, amplified in its weirdness because such a place should never be that quiet. I thought of Danny Beakerman and how I'd been desperate to taste the tiniest bit of him, carry something of him with me when he disintegrated from the world. I even thought to mention Regan, Eddie's officemate.

Instead I shook my head. "I'm boring, I guess. No evaporations for me."

The lie broke whatever spell was keeping them there, and everyone gathered up their things and made for the door. I yelled for them to remember to do the reading on de Kooning and Rothko and Lee Krasner for Thursday, but my voice had gone weirdly hoarse. I felt a brief wave of heat in my throat and wondered, with trembly fingers and my heart racing, if I was about to vanish. But then I was just alone in the room, the only sound my breathing and the ticking clock.

‡

I managed to fire two dozen dwarves by the time Eddie found me. My hands were chapped and dry and two of my fingernails were threatening to split.

"There you are," he said. He glanced at the dwarves, whose features were blank and beige, their eyes vacant. "These are creepy, all lined up like this."

"They're better when they have color."

"And when will that happen?"

"Tomorrow, I hope."

"I still think it's too much."

"It's something," I said. I didn't mention the change in her order. "How was your day?"

"Terrible. My students didn't do the reading." Eddie was teaching three courses, two creative writing classes and a course called "First Year Experience," which was a one-semester writing-intensive course required of all freshman. The topic he'd chosen was The Roaring Twenties, which he thought they would love, but as I'd joked when the semester started, not everyone loved Gatsby or jazz. "What about you?"

I started gathering my things, leaving the dwarves because I knew no one would take them. "Pretty good. My students wanted to talk about evaporations."

"How'd that come up?"

"It just did."

We ordered out again, salty Chinese from the buffet we'd been told was the best in town. When we got to the fortune cookies, Eddie shook his head, saying he wasn't in the mood for silly prophecies, so I forewent mine as well. Except later that night, when he'd fallen asleep, I found mine where I'd secreted it in the utensil drawer: *Adore what is there before it is gone.*

‡

The woman sent another email. *My wife's favorite colors were red and blue. I know it's kind of plain, but how can you fault someone for such simplicity? We slept on blue sheets, and she had red bath towels. Her favorite cup? Royal blue. Her favorite blanket? Cerulean. We played Clue all the time, and she was always Miss Scarlet. I think she was sad if either she or Mrs. Peacock was the killer. Her favorite memory was us going on vacation to the beach, because one morning the sunrise was that fiery red that means something to sailors, and the way it pressed against the clean blue of the ocean made her suck in a breath in a way I'd never heard before.*

I didn't respond; I didn't know what to say. I didn't delete the email, though, nor did I share it with Eddie; I could tell it was the kind of thing he'd frown at. By the end of the week I was nearly finished with the order, my fingers raw, nails caked with clay that I pried out every evening with a toothpick, leaving flecks behind in the bathroom sink. I stared down at them, as if they were the last bits of something I was washing away.

Eddie suggested Padilla's on Friday, and even though I was tired, and probably could have used the evening in the studio to finish the dwarves, I said yes. The parking lot was surprisingly full.

I don't know what I expected as we walked inside. Some sign of the evaporation, maybe. The space cordoned off by yellow tape, or an understood invisible barrier, people knowing not to step foot on that part of the floor. But everything was as it normally was: the pool tables were in full use; the booths were packed; Crosby, Stills, and Nash was blasting from the speakers. Both bars were jammed, drinkers shoulder-to-shoulder trying to get the bartenders' attention. I couldn't even quite remember where the man had evaporated. The only thing I noticed different was that Lake was not at her usual post; she had swapped, was fulfilling requests for mixed drinks at the liquor bar while someone else handled all the beer taps and bottles.

Eddie shoved his way into the pack to get us drinks while I kept an eye out for a place to sit. More students were around than usual.

"It's crowded," I said when Eddie returned with beers.

"Maybe because of the evaporation."

I'd been thinking the same, but I said, "Why would that bring in a crowd?"

Eddie shrugged. "A fascination, I guess."

"Do you find them fascinating?"

"I think they're just a part of life."

I frowned. A trio of guys in Stetsons stood up from a nearby booth, taking their beer bottles with them as they settled at a newly-available pool table, so I scuttled over to it, tugging on Eddie's shirtsleeve, and we slipped in. Eddie let out a sigh, as if he'd spent the day working on his feet instead of hunched over essays. My hands were throbbing and dry and I pressed them onto the tabletop, the skin taut and threatening to crack. He looked down at them and then rummaged in his pocket, extracting a travel-size bottle of Jergens lotion. He slid it across the table like he was playing shuffleboard.

"You brought this for me?"

"For both of us. The weather's been dry."

"I didn't know your skin got dry. You always feel moist to me."

Eddie opened his mouth to speak but then just laughed and drank from his beer. I poured what must have been half of the tiny bottle into my palms. The relief was immediate.

I felt my phone vibrate in my pocket, but I waited until Eddie went to the bathroom to check it: another email from the dwarf woman. I scrolled through the message fast. Another rejoinder about her dead wife, this time a story of how when they once went to Germany they drove from Frankfurt to Geratal just to go to a museum full of yard gnomes. She described the shelves and the displays, the endless array of gnomes and dwarves in various states of repose. How the museum smelled of paint and soil and kiln-fired clay, descriptions I had a hard time believing because, once they were set, such materials would barely give off a detectable odor. I slid my phone back in my pocket before Eddie returned.

"It's weird," he said upon his return.

"What is?"

Eddie settled himself in the booth, rocking his weight back and forth before taking a sip of his beer. "Just that, you know, there's no real evidence that anyone disappeared."

"I guess people move on quickly," I said, thinking of Danny Beakerman. How, yes, for a few weeks school was covered in a pall of mourning, even the most rambunctious class clowns muted in the hallways. Our teachers were in something of a stupor as they taught. Every sporting event started with a moment of silence. A few kids taped pictures of Danny up on their lockers and some of the bulletin boards. But then, as the weeks passed, people readjusted. Goofing and laughter filled the cafeteria again. The swim team, which hadn't met to go over summer training schedules, started up again. I stared down at the water in the pool, imagining that bits of Danny were still there. I ran my tongue over my lips and teeth, as if I could still taste whatever I might have swallowed down weeks prior. Eventually it was as if he'd never vanished, or, perhaps, had never existed in the first place.

"I think it's easier when you don't really know a person," Eddie said, gesturing toward the bar. "What was that man to us?"

"He was something to someone," I said.

"But not us."

"But not us, sure. But to all these people who are here that usually aren't?"

"Like I said." Eddie paused to drink. "A fascination."

We didn't stay long; the place was crowded, and we were both tired. As soon as we slid from our booth, strangers gestured and asked if we were leaving. I nodded, and they took our place, as if we had never been there. We threaded through the crowd, Eddie's hand in mine. I didn't allow myself to look back at the spot where the man had evaporated, still not sure I had the location right.

The night had gone cool. Eddie drove home with the windows open, a chilly breeze blasting our faces. He wanted to open the bedroom window and let the sounds of night come clattering in. We had found a place close to campus, and so the sidewalks on weekend nights were often filled with drunk students party-hopping. Their voices filled our bedroom, their boozy laughter and loud chatter an unexpected salve. I realized then, as Eddie kissed my throat, the air cutting across my naked back, that I liked where we were, that I was happy in a small college town. My hands were still dry and chapped, and when Eddie squeezed my fingers they flared with pain, but I didn't ask him to stop. I wanted that hurt. I needed it. The dwarves would be done soon, and, with the prospect of empty mornings and afternoons, I needed something to take their place. Pain was as good as anything, so long as it was something.

Eddie's tongue was hot on my skin. I could smell the beer on his breath, even though he'd only had two. He grunted and nudged me, so I turned onto my back and let his weight press down on me. Without a word, I let him in, let him do what he wanted. There was adoration in his breathing, in the press of his hips against mine. I closed my eyes, tasted salt, felt the air on my stomach, and prayed that, for as long as this lasted, I would still be around to feel it all.

CLINGING

The girls at the back of the church couldn't stop whispering to one another when Mrs. Schiffer, wife of their now-dead high school principal, grew her first set of roots right then and there in the middle of the funeral. The service had been going on for nearly thirty minutes at that point, and Natalie, Bea, and Noon were sure they weren't the only ones to notice. In fact, the whispers had begun four days ago, through the halls and in the cafeteria ever since Mr. Schiffer suffered a heart attack during that day's second period. Mrs. Schiffer, who had worked as his secretary for ten years before quitting to start a small bakery that parents frequented out of obligation more than any real love for the apple pies, had yet to grow any roots. So when they finally sprouted while the priest's baritone voice proclaimed how many students' lives her husband had touched, Natalie, Bea, and Noon couldn't help point it out to one another, their hands drifting toward their own heads almost unconsciously, fingers dusting against the roots there.

Natalie, of course, had the most prominent set, what with the horrible car crash that took the lives of her parents and younger twin brothers. They had been on the way to pick her up from summer camp. Her roots circled her head, the ones for her parents more pronounced than for Tim and Todd, something she felt bad about, but what can you do? You grieve for who you grieve for, she often said with a shrug.

Bea, on the other hand, felt a certain pride for the single tall stalk that emerged from the center of her scalp, parting her hair like an obelisk: for her grandmother, the only real caregiver she'd ever known, who had loved and raised Bea since her mother and father ran off when Bea was nothing more than a fleshy body in a bassinet, a wormy thing that cried for milk and warmth and the sound of a heartbeat. Her parents had come home after the grandmother's death, but their heads were smooth and glossy, which only made Bea angry.

Then, of course, Noon, with her many small lumps, more like bumps from smashing her head against the undersides of chairs or tables than roots proper: she hadn't ever seen or suffered the pain of a real loss, but tended to find herself shattered like a dropped plate at every tragedy imaginable. Once while she, Bea, and Natalie watched television, a character's pet rat kicked the bucket and another bulb popped up on Noon's head. Natalie and Bea stared at her, their mouths crowded with popcorn. They wondered aloud if something wasn't wrong with Noon, if she suffered some disease that made her too empathetic.

"You can't be too empathetic," Noon said.

"I think your head begs to differ. You look like a sea urchin," Bea said, through a mouthful of kernels.

"I can't help if I care so much."

Some truth to that, of course: no one could decide what stirred the deep sadness of loss. Mrs. Schiffer's bump-free head was no more her fault than Noon's crowded crown, and no more or less legitimate. The principal's wife had never felt true, unfiltered grief; Noon was wracked with it—or so it seemed—just about every day. Neither was better or worse than the other. Each one simply was.

As the funeral let out, Natalie said she was hungry, so she drove the three of them to a greasy diner a few blocks from school. They sat, Bea and Noon squashed together, in a booth facing the parking lot, with a wide, unblocked view of the street. As soon as their waitress passed them the flimsy, oversize menus, rain started spitting against the glass.

"Why do you think it took her so long?" Bea said. "You know, like, why not right when she heard he was dead?"

Natalie shrugged, trying to decide between a stack of pancakes and a patty melt. "I mean, maybe it just took that long for her to really feel like he was gone. Maybe she was in shock." Natalie thought of her own parents and brothers, the feeling that had hovered behind her eyes for weeks, a numbing like going to the dentist and being shot up with a tropical-tasting anesthetic in your gums so your tongue felt like a bloated armature poking at your gums and the dark cavern of your mouth.

She swallowed, the tip of her tongue tracing the lines of her palate.

Deciding on the pancakes, Natalie set down the menu and looked at the counter, trying to catch a glimpse of Paul Wilker, the basketball star who was also a line cook, through the swinging door leading to the grill and pots of brewing coffee. Natalie had gone on one date with him three weeks ago, and she'd kissed him on her front porch before her aunt flicked on the light above them. The kiss was good, made Natalie's body feel like a receding ocean, and she'd pressed her hand around Paul's bicep, which wasn't huge but compact, like a strong tube of dense sand. The golden hairs on his forearm had stood up like a crowd waving at her. His hair was short and cropped like an army infantryman's, revealing the two roots that swirled up along the crown of his head in a tall, craggy cowlick. For his grandparents, he'd explained on the way to the movies. They'd lived in his house for all of Paul's life in an apartment above the garage, his grandmother baking spanakopita every Saturday morning and making the house smell like spinach. They'd died days after one another, and Paul's grief for the one had seeped into the other. The sadness in Paul's voice when he told her echoed and caught between Natalie's ribs, and when she kissed him later that night she felt it pass from his

27

mouth to hers, and the sadness made her shiver, a tingling that ran from the back of her neck at her hairline down to the small of her back, and she'd been about to let her hands drift from Paul's arm toward his waist, her fingers insistent and filled with a desire to tug at the material of his jeans, when the light had snapped on, a momentary blindness that sucked the energy back out of her and into Paul.

"Did you hear the rumor about Gretchen Keohane?" Noon said. "Marcia Pallard told me that some of Gretchen's are fake."

The waitress appeared and took their order, gathering up the menus.

"Everyone's heard that rumor," Natalie said.

"But do you think it's true?" Bea said.

"No, I don't. Who would do that?"

"It's like putting on makeup though, isn't it?" Noon said, twirling a strand of her blue-black hair between her fingers.

"Pretending you have something to seriously mourn is not the same as hiding your pimples." Natalie craned her neck as the waitress pushed through the kitchen door, which swung with a creak and revealed a flash of the buttery kitchen. No sign of Paul. It did not occur to Natalie that of course Paul would not be working at eleven-thirty on a Wednesday, when Natalie herself would normally be planted in Algebra II, learning the foundations of trigonometry, were it not for the day of freedom afforded because of the death of her principal. This did finally occur to her right as she asked their waitress if Paul was working when she brought their food, Natalie's pancakes fluffy and thick and the size of dinner plates. She felt a flash of embarrassed stupidity, not only for her thoughtlessness but also for even mentioning Paul, which elicited giggling snickers from Bea and Noon when their waitress waddled off to refill the maple syrup dispenser whose sticky lid didn't want to open.

"You want to have sex with him, don't you?" Noon said.

"I do not," Natalie said. "And even if I did, that is not your business."

"That's a yes," Bea said, elbowing Noon and chortling. The noise made Natalie think of a pig snarfling on its gruel. She rolled her eyes and unfurled her knife and fork from their cinched blanket of napkin.

"I wonder if I'll ever have any like Mrs. Guilford. Hers are huge, like tree branches," Bea said, between bites, lifting her hand eighteen inches over her head and letting it hover there like a watchful billboard.

"But then you might have to shave your head like she does." Noon swallowed a forkful of runny eggs. "And, really, can you imagine having three husbands die like that? All in car accidents, right before you're supposed to have a baby every time?"

The thought of Mrs. Guilford, their history teacher, walking through her front door every afternoon to three mismatched children, all crowing for their fathers and snacks, made Natalie's stomach flop. She pushed her pancakes away and stared out the window, watching cars shoot by, their colors blurred by the rain thickening on the glass. A weight seemed to be settling in her chest, and she wanted nothing more than for Paul Wilker to appear and root around inside her and remove whatever was sinking into her. She felt a tightness atop her head, her roots stretching just so. They did this now and then, their cedar toughness pulling at her scalp when she thought of other peoples' plight.

Noon, who asked Natalie if she still wanted the rest of her pancakes as she sank her fork into the stack, didn't notice. But Bea set her knife down and laid a finger on Natalie's wrist. She narrowed her eyes and gave Natalie a once-over, asking if she was okay.

Natalie stared back. Bea's hair was a frizzy auburn that she liked to twirl up into a fifties-style beehive around the thick root that stuck out like a lightning rod. She had freckles to match, which darkened when she was embarrassed.

"I guess," Natalie said. "I don't think I'm hungry after all."

They paid, leaving a generous tip as Natalie's aunt had taught her to always do, and clambered into Natalie's car. Bea gave Noon the front seat and chuffed into the empty space behind the driver's seat, Natalie's textbooks and a pile of athletic shorts and sports bras occupying the other side. Natalie could sense Bea staring at the back of her head, and she resisted the urge to pat at her roots. Natalie's were casually attractive adornments, shaped almost like a wreath of laurels around the back of her head, cradling the swaths of her hair like a bird's nest. Natalie kept her hair short around the sides but let the locks below her roots grow, and she usually looped them up and over the tendrils gathered there, a small poncho of hair to protect them from the elements. But today her hair was loose, the roots exposed.

The rain was heavy but cool, so they sat on Bea's screened-in porch and read magazines, skimming over 100 tips for pleasing your man, guffawing at the suggestions about what to do to his penis and scrotum. None of them had seen a boy naked in person, Noon coming the closest, having glimpsed her father a few times when she was a kid and they had only one bathroom in a clapboard apartment that smelled like Swiss cheese and car exhaust. They'd taken sex ed and had to look at the pictures, cartoonish artists' renditions of the human anatomy, the parts labeled and distinguished in garish pink, purple, and orange swatches, and had tried to imagine what excitement there could be in letting one of their stinking male classmates put that in them, anywhere, and Bea and Noon giggled and slapped at each other. Natalie kept picturing Paul Wilker, tall and lithe and sinewy. Sometimes he didn't wear a shirt while shooting hoops at the public court near her house and she would stroll by, his skin glowing in the sunlight. His hip bones jutted out like the lips of a vase, pointing toward his center, and when Natalie thought of it she wanted to see what was beyond his swishing mesh shorts, a heat rising in her cheeks that she tried to stanch. She pictured herself lying on the white sheets of her bed, Paul towering above her, his shorts flapping like ribbon, her hands parting the scrunched band of material at his waist, the skin near his groin dark and tender, coarse pubic hair like a welcome mat.

Bea's mother, arriving home from her day working as a bank teller, offered to order the girls a pizza for dinner. Bea rolled her eyes and coughed up a sighed *whatever*, giving no response to her mother's inquiry about toppings. Noon suggested bacon, and Natalie shrugged assent. Bea acted as if she'd heard none of it, and her mother let the door into the house swing shut.

"Jeez," Bea said, tossing the magazine onto the frosted-glass table. "She just doesn't get it."

"She's trying," Natalie said.

"I know, but she thinks pizza can fix everything."

"I kinda think it can," Noon said. "Especially when topped with bacon."

Bea rolled her eyes, which made Natalie clench her fists. Whenever Bea hemmed and huffed about her mother, Natalie wanted to punch her. What Natalie wouldn't do to have her parents back, offering to order pizza, working long hours to give her and her friends a screened-in porch on which to sit in the afternoon after going to a funeral. She rubbed the nylon material of her dress between her fingers and willed the tension in her knuckles to subside. Natalie thought of Paul, the relaxed heft of his hands against her hips, the soft way his fingertips had palmed her skin when they kissed, like she was a basketball he was bouncing with weightless ease.

While they ate their pizza, the noise of laughter rose through the bushes that separated Bea's yard from the Thompsons' next door, and two of them, the twins who were the eldest of four, emerged, waving at the girls. They stopped before the screen door, rapping on the plastic frame. None of the girls moved to open it.

"Hey," one of them, Donny, said.

Natalie glanced toward Bea, who smirked toward Donny Thompson. Bea's crush on Donny, a baseball player with sandy hair that was verging on too long, was no secret to Noon or Natalie or, Natalie thought, Donny himself. Bea admired him from afar, waving at him and cheering during baseball games she dragged Natalie and Noon to so she could fawn over him from the bleachers while Natalie developed sunburn on her shoulders. He was, Natalie had to admit, good-looking, if a bit stupid. Well-intentioned, quieter than the rest of his teammates and certainly the most human of his brood. The Thompsons were known for their wildness, Donny's twin brother Will having already gotten in trouble for drinking himself stupid last summer and hotwiring Mr. Schiffer's car. He got nowhere on his joyride, bonking into a car parked across the street as he reversed out of the principal's driveway too fast. Donny and Will's younger brothers, eleven and ten, didn't bathe, so the rumor went, except on Sunday nights when their mother, an exhausted, frumpy woman, finally broke down and cried, like clockwork, begging the boys into the bathtub where a week's worth of grime and silt turned the water to brackish soup in seconds, the boys coming out several pounds lighter. Their basement, where Donny and Will slept, smelled like the ocean and dirty socks.

"Hey," Donny said again, letting his arm fall.

"What do you want?" Bea said, not looking at him.

"Just wanted to offer you ladies an invite. Party at our house Friday."

"Oh yeah?" Bea flicked her fingertips with her tongue and turned the page of her magazine, propping her feet on the table. Her dress slid up her legs, revealing the snow white of her upper thighs.

"Yeah," Donny said while Will stared stupidly at Bea's skin. Natalie felt herself tense at his slovenly gaze, imagining Paul drumming his fingers over her. He'd set his hand on Natalie's knee during the movie, but his fingers had remained statue-like.

She'd felt the weight of his skin sinking into hers. Paul removed them when the credits rolled and shoved his hands in his pockets when they stood to leave.

"Well, okay," Bea said. "We could come over, I guess. Seems a bit early to be planning, doesn't it?"

Donny's mouth broke into a smile like a safe cracked by a robber. "Well, we want everyone to have plenty of notice." He winked, then turned away. Will followed him to the brush, then Donny stopped so fast they bumped shoulders. "Hope you don't have plans."

"Mmm hmm," Bea said.

Natalie watched the Thompsons push the brush out of the way. Their heads were rounded and smooth; Will's hair was cropped close to the scalp so it stood like a brush's bristles. Neither of them had any roots, as if their lives were absent of worry, scrubbed clean of the tangling feelings of loss.

‡

On Friday Natalie met Noon at Bea's house and they stood in Bea's bathroom, cycling around one another as they applied make-up and fixed their hair. Bea went through four different outfits, Natalie and Noon insisting that any of them would do. Natalie had chosen jeans and the t-shirt she'd worn on her date with Paul, with whom she had still not spoken even though she'd caught sight of him at the basketball court on Thursday after school. Noon wore a sundress that accentuated the shape of her attractive shoulders, which were neither bony nor muscular nor fat, but some eye-catching combination of all three, reminiscent of stones washed by rushing water.

They marched down the sidewalk behind a cluster of boys from school whose names they did not know. Although their high school was moderate in size, their class three hundred people, Natalie made it her business to willfully ignore the names of those who annoyed her, including the entire cheerleading squad and the overly-prim girls who took all honors courses and sang in the school choir. Bea and Noon had taken up a similar tack, though Natalie was certain, based on the quantity and urgency of the gossip they shared every day, that they mostly pretended not to know who people were whereas Natalie really did have a void in her brain where most of her peers' names belonged.

The Thompson house was already crowded when the girls arrived, the air in the foyer sour with the smell of teenage bodies, natural acrid odors covered by floral perfumes and colognes splashed egregiously along necks and wrists. Deodorant smeared over armpits was unsuccessful in keeping up with the sweat forming on bodies and in the tangles of newly-sprouted body hair. The house was damp. Natalie forged ahead through the crowd, parting people like waves, Noon and Bea slinking through in her wake.

In Natalie's estimation, two groups of teenage girls existed: first, those who flaunted their roots, like Gretchen Keohane, who was dancing on the Thompsons' coffee table and holding a red cup of some drink over her head. It sloshed over the halter top that barely covered her chest and revealed a sparkling belly button ring that must have been fake. And second, girls like Natalie, who tended to cover their roots; her hair, that night, was draped up high on her head in a pseudo-chignon. Natalie preferred members of the latter group, the ones who held their grief close and thought it a personal accessory, like a tattoo drawn across the inner lip or thigh, revealed as a matter of necessity rather than pride.

She led Noon and Bea into the kitchen, where every surface was crowded with crumpled Dixie cups, empty beer bottles, and towering handles of cheap rum and vodka, the laminate countertop smeared in a layer of spilled liquor and Kool-Aid. Donny Thompson stood next to a keg, shirtless, a red mesh trucker's hat tilted backward on his head, his thick, young muscles twitching as he pumped beer into a girl's cup. He caught sight of the three of them and waved them over. Bea practically stampeded to him. Natalie sidestepped, turning her shoulder into the back of someone standing around the greasy kitchen island, and left Bea to fawn over Donny with Noon at her side. Natalie needed to pee.

The Thompson house was foreign to her, the hallways dark and all of the doors closed. She tried one and found a tired laundry room with wrinkled, wet clothes hanging from a wire shelf. A fat cat howled when she opened the door and it darted out. Natalie watched as the cat froze at the din before it, unsure of what to do in the mess of sloppy teenagers and pounding music. Then, bristling, the cat took off toward the stairs leading to the basement. Natalie continued her search, interrupting two couples in bedrooms—one of them Will Thompson and a suddenly-relocated Gretchen Keohane, whose shirt was off, half of her sizable chest covered by Will's squeezing hand—until she finally discovered a half-bath. She shut the door and sat down on the closed toilet, her need to urinate suddenly gone. Natalie rubbed her eyes and stretched her neck so she could see her face in the mirror, trying to remove the image of half-naked Gretchen from her brain. Gretchen's lips had been draped open while Will sucked at her neck and earlobe, her head thrown back so her blonde hair dribbled toward the small of her back. As Natalie had backed out of the room, Gretchen let out a small peep of excitement.

Natalie checked her own hair and pried her phone from her pocket: nothing. She'd sent Paul Wilker a message about the party that afternoon, wondering if he would be here, but he hadn't replied. Natalie had spent the afternoon wondering what she could have done wrong, reliving their kiss. Maybe he'd found her lips too dry. Or perhaps too wet. The temptation to send him another message asking if he was in the Thompsons' house drilled at her like a cracked tooth, but she slid her phone away in her pocket and left the bathroom.

The humidity of the hallway hit her like a sack of flour, leaving her unbalanced and dizzy even though Natalie hadn't had a single drink. She felt disoriented, and, though intending to return to the kitchen in the hope of finding Noon and Bea, turned the wrong way and found herself at the cracked doorway of the master bedroom.

And perched on the edge of the bed, which she could see in the open sliver between door and frame, was Paul Wilker, embracing another member of the basketball team, their hands on each other's arms, lips locked together. Because of the music pumping up from somewhere beneath them, neither of the boys heard Natalie's footsteps or caught the slight wheeze the door gave when she pushed it open just so.

The light was dim, one solitary lamp on a bedside table casting most of the room in shadow, but Natalie could see the contour of the boys' bodies and, more importantly, the way they held each other. The touch of their lips was filled with an electric want, their fingers light and thorough at the same time, like thrusting one's hand through sand on a beach. Natalie didn't recognize the boy kissing Paul, his unkempt blonde hair, wide jaw, peach-pink skin all unfamiliar. But the yearning she could see in the way their bodies touched, how both of their eyes were shut in relaxed darkness, was plain and screeching to her: she recognized, with an exacting ache, the way she'd leaned into Paul, the senseless, upside-down feeling she'd experienced when they had latched onto each other. The memory flashed through her brain: the touch of Paul's lips, his drawn-back shoulders, and she was filled with the realization that Paul Wilker had not felt the same thing as her when they had kissed.

Natalie backed away. She stood still, frozen by the laughter and cacophony of the party. For a moment she was immersed in the darkness of the hall, underwater. Then she turned and made her way back toward the kitchen, where she would find Bea and Noon. They would look at her for a moment, sensing that something was wrong, but she would shake them off and smile, ask for Bea to gather a cup for her from Donny Thompson.

They would settle at a low table in the living room and play a drinking game where Natalie would catch the attention of the boys around her. She would smile at them, bat her eyes, make them wonder and hope, but she would ultimately break their hearts, stumbling down the sidewalk at the end of the night with Noon and Bea in tow, the latter complaining about not hooking up with Donny Thompson who, according to Bea, had the body of a god. He should be carved into marble, she would warble, stumbling into the grass. Noon would help her up while Natalie smiled with a soft sadness.

All of that would come soon. But as she slid down the hall, avoiding the electric touch of her classmates, she reached toward the center of her scalp, where she felt a bump: a root breaking through her skin, a tiny lump that she willed to become nothing more than a blip, something no one else but she would know was there, something Natalie would have no trouble hiding.

HOLLOWED GROUNDS

After our mother died, my sister and I couldn't agree on when to let our parents' house ascend. Kirstie wanted to let it go right away, only days after the funeral. I said no; there was still tons of stuff to go through.

"Like what?" she said. "What could be so important?"

We were sitting in the dining room of her apartment, which was small and stuffy and smelled like stale smoke. The landlord had promised my sister when she took a tour that cleaners would take care of the odor, but there it had been when she moved in.

I told her that there were things like their keepsakes, our mom's jewelry, our dad's ties. And the refrigerator was still full.

"What?" she said. "You want our mother's milk?"

I told her that was a gross way to put that.

"It's gross that you think I'm being gross."

I said it was gross that she didn't want to keep any of our parents' things. I said that floating everything into the sky was cruel.

"They're dead," Kirstie said. "They don't care."

But I did, I said. She rolled her eyes and leaned back in her chair. All of Kirstie's furniture was ramshackle and tired, found on street corners during neighborhood spring cleanings and in the dusty, untouched corners of consignment stores. None of the chairs matched; she was sitting in a wicker monstrosity that creaked every time she moved. The arms were fraying and would grab at your clothing and skin as you walked by if you weren't careful. My chair was wooden, the kind of thing you'd find at a church picnic under the central tent where fried chicken was served and live music made talking impossible.

Kirstie yawned. "Okay. How about this: you take two weeks to do whatever you want. Then we send it skyward."

Her face was stiff. Where my features were all scrubby and unremarkable, Kirstie's were hard. Her cheekbones gathered all the light they encountered. Her eye sockets were huge, like she was undernourished. She had recently dyed her hair the deepest shade of black I'd ever seen, and when she ran her fingers through it, the pink of her nails was a shock.

I said fine.

"Okay. Sounds like a plan," she said, standing and walking into the kitchen. While she was cantilevered over her open fridge looking for a snack, she added, "Don't get sucked up along with it. That would be a pain in my ass."

‡

When Schimmer set the amaretto sour in front of me he leaned forward, elbows on the bar. He was dressed in his usual uniform: a crisp white Oxford with the sleeves rolled up to show off the interstate of veins in his forearms, a pair of suspenders that held up his tight black pinstripe pants and pinched the fabric of his shirt; and a red bowtie that looked like something Ronald McDonald would wear.

I told him thanks and he smiled, waiting for me to take a sip. He didn't make his amarettos with sour mix, instead using egg whites for the foam and a simple syrup, the whiskey killing off anything that might give a drinker stomach problems. As a result, they tasted less cloying than most cocktails, and I, who didn't like sweet, could drink them.

"So," he said after I'd taken my first sip. "How are you?"

I told him about Kirstie's deadline.

Schimmer nodded but didn't say anything; he had to shuffle down to the other end of the bar where a trio of women in their forties had taken up residence. I recognized them; they came into Mikey's for trivia every Tuesday night, mostly getting last place as they laughed at their own ignorance about world geography and American history. Sometimes I played, filling half of the answer sheet, leaving anything I wasn't sure about blank; Schimmer would come by and whisper answers to me, his lips near my ear. The women would glance my way and smile.

When he came back after pouring their pitcher of beer and a trio of Washington Apple shots, he said, "I could come help. If that would help. Have someone detached from things look at them."

I told him I would think about it. He had sent his parents' house up two years prior, a fact he shared when I told him I was worried about my mom, that her decline into early-onset Alzheimer's was picking up speed. She'd shouted at Kirstie and tried to bite her home health aide twice in the same day. Kirstie and I knew the prognosis. It had kept me up at night.

"It wasn't easy at first," he admitted when we talked about it. "Seeing it disappear into the clouds. But then there was a feeling that I could move on. I couldn't dwell because, well, it wasn't there anymore to dwell on. Or in."

I nodded. My father had died when I was a senior in college, a freak accident at the meat processing plant where he'd worked my entire life, first on the floor, and then as a manager. He was the good sort of supervisor, who returned to his laborer roots whenever someone called in sick or the company was short-staffed. That kindness had been repaid by the Ultrex processor malfunctioning, a piece of steel careening off the machine and into my father's temple. Only six months later, my mother started showing signs of dementia, and although her neurologist said it was a coincidence, I was never fully convinced that her debilitation wasn't a direct result of losing my dad. Kirstie went through her own six-month period of barely eating, her wrist bones popping, clavicle rising up to prominence. She eventually started eating again, but my mother never recovered.

The women at the end of the bar always begged Schimmer to help them with the questions they didn't know the answers to. He always gave them a Cheshire grin and didn't acquiesce, playing stupid. His first name was Michael, but he went by his last because he didn't want people thinking he was the owner; no one affiliated with Mikey's was actually named Mikey. No one, not even the owner, had any idea why that was what the bar was called—it had changed hands several times over the years thanks to the economic crisis of the early 2000s—but no one had changed the name.

Some nights, I stuck around after trivia was over to help Schimmer close, or at least wait for him to finish wiping down the bar and restocking the beer cooler. That night I didn't, closing out my tab—he only charged me for one amaretto even though I nursed my way through two—as soon as trivia was over; the women came in last, as usual. Schimmer didn't try to persuade me to stick around, setting down the duplicates of my credit card slip with a pen he pulled from his pocket. I always tipped way too much, at least according to him, but I didn't care, especially now. My mother had an excellent life insurance policy, and she had also been flush with cash from the wrongful death suit following my father's accident. Though I wouldn't be buying a mansion anytime soon, I could afford to dole out excessive tips to whomever I wanted.

When he saw the number on the topmost slip, Schimmer pursed his lips but didn't say anything. He simply picked up the papers and my empty glass and then wiped down my spot. By the time I was out the door, the women noisily chirping for another round, all evidence I'd been there was gone.

‡

The first house I saw ascend in person was the Van Dillons' across the street. The family had been struck by tragedy, four out of the five members killed in a freak car crash as they made their way from Missouri to the east coast for a vacation at Myrtle Beach. I was friends with Nicholas, the eldest of the three kids and the sole survivor. We were fourteen and in the same physical science and freshman English classes. Something had happened as the family traversed the mountains involving a runaway semi-truck and failed brakes. Nicholas was in the hospital in Charlotte for weeks before he was able to fly home. A sister and brother-in-law of the deceased Mrs. Van Dillon came to empty the house, clearing out most of it before Nicholas was released, his broken leg and sutured face still healing. I witnessed his arrival, watching from our front window, a bay identical to one that bumped out from the Van Dillon home. Nicholas climbed out of a town car, his uncle gripping his elbow as he limped in through the garage, which had already been cleared of his father's tools. He stared at the bare walls, the empty power outlets, the desolate work bench. I couldn't see the look on his face, but I felt a pinching pain in my gut. Two mornings later he was gone, driven away early—the sound of car doors opening and closing in their driveway woke me—and then, later that afternoon, the house rose.

I'd watched video footage of ascensions, but like so many things, seeing it live was so different. The sound, first of all, was like nothing I'd heard before: though the house goes up in clean fashion, the pipes and cement and rebar do not. They resist and roar and screech; electrical wire twangs and frays where it's ripped apart. The foundation looks bulbous, cancered, a heavy cloud clinging to the bottom of the house. Front porch steps are a stuck-out tongue, as if the house is making a face as it rises into the clouds, leaving behind a puddled mess, the driveway pointing into a wretched abyss.

After the Van Dillon house rose, I walked over and stood at the end of the front walkway. Earthworms wriggled in the exposed soil. Pipes gaped like confused mouths. I could smell the dirt, the water. The septic tank was a bulging white bulb, its side exposed like pearly fat. I was tempted to climb down into the pit, but I heard my sister yelling from our house; she was still young enough not to be brash. I turned to her pleading voice and left the Van Dillon house behind. Years later, she would tumble into a similar crater with her first boyfriend. I asked her what it was like to be down there. She said, "Nothing special. All of the important stuff was gone."

‡

"Is it a money issue?" Kirstie said.

I turned around and told her she'd scared me. I was in our parents' bedroom, trying to sort through their clothes, something no one had done after our father died; his sports coats still smelled of his brut cologne. The master bedroom was home to a pair of closets, one for him and one for her, and I must have been pulling dresses from hangers when Kirstie walked into the house and called out for me, because I hadn't heard her.

I asked her what she meant by money issue.

She shrugged. "If we let the place ascend, we can't sell it."

I frowned and told her we could still sell the land. That, I said, was what most people did. I didn't add that it was common knowledge that houses in which people had died and that had not been sent into the sky had terrible market value: superstitions about hauntings. Kirstie knew this. I asked her again why she thought it was a money issue.

"I don't know. I don't know your finances."

I told her I was doing fine, which she should have known, and turned back to the pile of clothes. Our mother had liked empire line dresses, and the bed was heaped with rich fabrics, dark plum and scarlet colors that she said emphasized the alabaster of her skin in a way that didn't make her look sickly. Our father was a fan of pinstripe pants. I was having trouble sorting because I didn't actually know what the piles should be. Of course there was a pile to give away to Goodwill or whoever could make best use of things, but what to do with Neiman Marcus and Nordstrom dresses? What about a bespoke suit? Did one just give these things away? Should I have been trying to sell them? Did people hold onto their parents' formalwear?

If Kirstie was concerned about these questions, she didn't show it, plopping down on one of the heaps. She fiddled with the straps of one of our mother's dresses. She twiddled the fabric between her thumbs and said nothing. Then she let go of the dress and patted it like she was trying to comfort a child.

"Need any help?"

I asked her why she wanted to help if she was ready to let it all go.

"Jesus, Christian."

I stared at her.

"Fine," she said, standing. "Forget I asked."

I asked her why she'd come over in the first place.

"I just wanted to check in. We haven't talked in a few days."

I frowned, said that wasn't unusual.

"Our mother just died. That makes it unusual." She shook her head. "Does that not make sense to you?"

I said that everything made sense in the immediate aftermath of death. And that nothing made sense, either.

"Well, that's poetic." She let out a huff of air. "I just want to get this done, okay?"

I asked her if she was already ready to move on.

"I have been for a while," she said. Kirstie was looking toward the open bedroom door. "It's impressive you haven't."

I wanted to ask her why she thought I wasn't ready to move on, but I couldn't think of how to word it; the idea stuck in my throat, a thick clog. By the time I felt able to speak, she was halfway down the hall, and I didn't have it in me to call for her to come back.

‡

Schimmer had shaved. He'd nicked the side of his throat. I asked him what had happened and he said, "Unsteady hands."

When I asked why unsteady, he shrugged and said, "You look terrible."

I had not been sleeping. As I moved through my parents' house, the task of going through their things seemed more and more onerous. Beyond their clothing there were all of their bathroom essentials, my father's collection of watches—much larger than I'd ever known—and their endless supply of dinnerware and extra bedding. My mother had bought a decade's worth of Christmas wrap and ornaments, a dozen new stockings. Kirstie's childhood bedroom closet still held a number of her old toys, Barbie dolls and Matchbox cars crammed into plastic tubs that were stacked next to an array of unused winter coats. When I told her about them she laughed and said, "Well, those you can send right up into the sky."

Schimmer set a shot glass in front of me and filled it with expensive tequila. He slid it my way and said nothing. He knew I didn't do straight shots, and I knew he knew. He knew that I knew he knew, but he smirked at me anyway, waiting. The women were already squawking in preparation for trivia. I took the shot, shivering as its turpentine taste slithered down my throat. When Schimmer made a move to pour another, I overturned the glass and shook my head.

"It'd do you some good," he said.

I told him no thanks, but then when I came back from the bathroom later, the shot glass was full again. He said nothing about it, nor did he remind me of his offer to help, and when Schimmer moved away to pour another pitcher of beer for the women, I drank it.

The ladies got last place again, laughing when the emcee announced the scores. This week's questions were harder than usual, it seemed, topics like the history of Albanian princes and esoteric 1960s movies, but that may have been because I felt like I was swimming underwater thanks to the shots. I sipped my amaretto slowly. I stuck around when the bar emptied even though I was exhausted. When closing time arrived, I helped Schimmer clean, but my limbs were loose and weird and I couldn't really lift the bar stools, and when I tried to sweep, I kept missing the discarded swizzle sticks and ripped-apart paper coasters that one table had left beneath their seats in a fuzzy drizzle. Schimmer laughed as he restocked the maraschino cherries and cut fresh limes for the next day, but then, when he was finally clocked out, he pulled me close to him as we walked out of the bar, his arm heavy on my shoulder. He smelled of fruited cologne and spicy aftershave. I reached up and poked at the dried blood on his throat and he didn't jerk away. He dumped me in the passenger seat of his car without a word and took me back to his apartment, an industrial-style loft with polished cement floors the color of caramelized sugar. His bedroom had exposed ductwork and our voices echoed like we were on the edge of the Grand Canyon; I wanted to yell something but couldn't think of what. While he brushed his teeth I stared up at the ceiling. When he came in from the bathroom in only his boxer shorts, I wanted to run my hands all over him, but when he pulled himself under the top sheet he pushed my hands away, telling me I was too drunk. I begged and pleaded but he said no, no. "In the morning, okay?"

I said okay.

When his colognes and deodorants were stripped away, Schimmer's body gave off a yeasty smell, like a brewery. As he slept—I couldn't ever fall asleep after drinking, the sour fruit of alcohol churning in my stomach—I pressed my face between his shoulder blades and took deep breaths. I read somewhere, once, that smell is our weakest sense but that it flares up the most powerfully in memory, and so I inhaled his odor with a taut, hard sense of urgency. I let my hand slide onto his hip as I inhaled.

After my father died, I felt him slipping away fast, as if it wasn't just my mother whose brain was betraying itself. I lost the sound of his voice, the shape of his eyes, the rattling noise of his footsteps. His laugh vanished quickly. I imagined my mother feeling the ground loosen beneath her, these most important pieces of the most important person in her life turning to amorphous jelly.

If Schimmer woke or noticed when I touched him, when I pulled in his scent, he gave no sign. I was grateful for this, for the way he allowed me to take from him, hold the smell of his skin and the feel of his flesh, anything to keep me grounded.

In the morning, he turned to me and smiled, kissing me hard on the lips, tongue pressing into my mouth despite my sour breath. Everything wasn't okay, but it felt better.

‡

After the Van Dillon house ascended, I would sometimes sneak out at night and stare into the empty pit. Pipes glistened. Standing water from summer rains shimmered. I thought I could hear the ghostly whispers of floorboards settling, even though there were no floorboards left. Eventually, on the cusp of school starting, I found some courage and descended into the maw that was the empty crater, using unearthed stones and left-behind splotches of concrete as footholds.

The odor of gas and soil was rich and thick. I felt like I was in a cavern. I could see stars, and I convinced myself that I could also see the outlines of hundreds, thousands, millions of ascended houses, though of course I could not. When they lifted into the air they sloughed up at a rough angle, tilting with the wind as if all that brick and metal was nothing more than rubber, plastic, paper. They grew smaller and smaller, becoming nothing more than a dot, and then, eventually, they vanished.

In the Van Dillon hole, I imagined the spot that would have been the basement. Nicholas and I had spent time there playing his Xbox and Nintendo 64; he was better at the former, me the latter, but we always played both in equal measure, and neither of us really ever got mad when we lost. The one time I beat him at Halo, Nicholas gave me a high-five. His hand was sweaty from gripping the controller, but our palms remained sealed together for a beat longer than normal. He looked away and finally withdrew his fingers, but I remembered that touch for a long time, wishing more than once that we could replicate it.

One day, I woke up to noise across the street: construction of a new house had begun. There'd been no for sale sign. But soon enough a foundation was poured, rebar and wooden joists embedded in the ground. The space I had stared down at was gone, a new set of lives ready to take its place. The new house was still standing strong when my father died, and then my mother. I never imagined it would outlast my childhood home.

‡

On Kirstie's assigned deadline day, she met me outside the house. She parked on the street, one block away.

"You ready for this?" she said. We stood shoulder-to-shoulder on the curb before the front walk.

I told her no.

She sighed. "I didn't think you'd be. Come on."

I asked her where we were going.

"Inside. I want you to show me what you still need to do."

I followed her; Kirstie still had a key, which I took as a sign that she'd known I wouldn't be ready. She unlocked the door in a fast, fluid motion, so quick she didn't even have to stop walking as she hopped up the single step onto the porch. Inside, she paused in the foyer and pulled open the coat closet, where our mother's heavy winter coat and two of our father's windbreakers still hung.

"We're off to a great start," she said.

I told her I'd forgotten about those.

The living room furniture was still where it had always sat, couch legs digging divots into the carpet.

I told her I thought maybe she'd want the couch and recliner, to replace the mishmash of her apartment.

"Why would I want to do that?" she asked. Then, before I could say anything in response, she noted the presence of the television and the photographs on the walls. "What exactly have you done over the last two weeks?"

I told her I felt like I'd done a lot. But also nothing. When we entered the kitchen and she saw that the cabinets were still half-full, she groaned and said, "You're just delaying the inevitable."

When I said I didn't think anything was inevitable, she stared at me.

"People die, Christian. We all do."

I didn't have anything to say to that.

The rest of the tour was uninspired. Kirstie stood, flummoxed, in every room. I saw evidence of my sorting, but even more evidence of what was holding on. No matter how hard I'd tried to excavate my parents and their things, the house still breathed them; the master bathroom smelled of my mother's perfumes, floral and citrusy; the office reeked of my father's cigar smoking, the one sin he committed that my mother couldn't forgive. I'd emptied his papers, at least, but the bookshelves were still half-full, as I couldn't bring myself to pull down the leather-bound first-editions he kept on a high built-in behind his desk. I had at least come close to emptying the basement, but that was because the contents was largely our childhood toys and stuffed animals and bins full of our college papers and grade school soccer trophies. My mother's plastic Christmas tree and the tangles of lights my father tried to fix every year instead of buying new ones were still in their boxes.

"Jeez," Kirstie said, trudging back into the living room. "Are you that desperate to keep the house?"

I asked her if she was that desperate for it to go.

We stared at one another like antagonists in a film that has reached its crescendo. Eventually, Kirstie plopped down on one of the sofas and seemed to crumple, spine curved inward, arms lazed down between her legs.

"Look," she said. "I don't know about you, but I don't want to grieve anymore."

I said, as gently as I could, that Mom had just died.

"She didn't even know who we were anymore."

I couldn't argue with this. I sat down next to Kirstie. For the first time I saw how tired she was; bruised-blue coronas surrounded her lower eyelids. Her lips were droopy. I put my arm around her but said nothing. She leaned into me. She smelled like peaches. We sat that way for a long time.

Near the end of her life, my mother would look out the living room window toward the house across the street. I found her that way once, and she wouldn't break her gaze no matter what I said or how loud I yelled. I called Kirstie, freaked out, and told her something was wrong. She came over, but by the time she arrived, my mother had snapped out of it. I told her I was sorry.

"Don't be sorry," she said, sighing. "Just don't scare me like that."

I spent that afternoon with my mother, who sat cheerfully in her recliner, watching talk shows and *Jeopardy!* as if nothing had happened. Mostly, I looked across the street at the neighbors' house, superimposing in my mind the Van Dillons' home, but I couldn't get it to appear correctly. Its gables and windowpanes and the color of the garage door had all disappeared from my memory. The realization made me queasy: how easy things could float away.

"Christian, please." Kirstie's voice shocked me: she was actually pleading. "I think I need this. I can't keep pretending they're still here."

I told her I wasn't pretending. I just wasn't ready to let their house, everything it meant, go.

All of a sudden, my sister was crying. The last time I'd seen her sob she was twelve and had broken her tibia after leaping from a swing on a playground. The sound was gnarled and harsh then; now, it was pillowy, soft. All pain, I thought, is different.

I tugged her to me. She sobbed into the soft space between my shoulder and chest. She didn't say anything when I stood and pulled her up with me. She still said nothing when I sidled us out the front door and onto the front stoop. When I turned us to face the house, she stopped crying, detangled herself from me and wiped her runny nose with the sleeve of her shirt. She let out a half-sob, half-laugh. I tried to laugh, but nothing came out. We both looked at the house, weighed down by our shared past. I stared, wondering what would happen. No matter which of us won, the truth was we had both lost. And nothing would change that, no matter who let go first.

FORGOTTEN FOLK

I

"Jan Frances."

"Oh, god. Jan Frances."

"I take it that means I win?" Cam was already rolling onto his stomach.

"Yes," I said, writhing like a salmon trying to drag itself upstream as I untangled myself from the sheets. "Jan Frances will do that."

Cam and I were playing Forgotten Folk: we each had ten seconds to muster up the name of some forgotten person from our past. The winner received a back massage. Jan Frances tried to give Cam a blowjob during senior prom, blitzing him in a dark corner of the gym where the temporary disco ball and laser lights couldn't reach. I'd been in the bathroom at the time, unloading a night's worth of punch into a urinal. She'd managed to unhook his cummerbund before I rescued him.

Cam laughed into his pillow. "Fuck. Jan Frances. Poor girl had no clue, Allen."

"Didn't she wear braces?" I said.

"No, that was Patricia Marques."

I pressed my hands into the center of Cam's back. Most former Division I athletes lose it after a few years out of college, but Cam's body was still hard and lined like a map full of highways. I didn't mind when he was the victor.

"Patricia also tried to give you a few blowjobs, I'm sure."

"She might have succeeded once."

I rolled my eyes before moving my hands onto the high ridge of his coccyx where it met the bulb of his glutes. I licked at his spine.

"That's not usually part of a back massage," Cam said.

The blinds were cinched shut, but through the darkness came a sudden flood of blue and red. Not wholly unusual in our neighborhood, not because our area was crime-riddled but because a fire station was situated down the street. At least a few times a month the crone of a siren pierced the night, emergency lights spangling our bedroom ceiling. I, at least, took comfort in knowing rescue was close by.

The light intensified and then stuck, static and shifty.

"Huh," I said, prying myself away from Cam and spearing my fingers through the blinds. "There's a cop car, an ambulance, and a fire truck at the Gettemeyers' house."

Cam flopped out of bed and we both pulled on boxers and t-shirts and slid into flip flops. When I pulled open the front door the August air was tumid and thick, like we were surrounded by a cavalry of creatures panting out heavy, wet breath.

Cam shaded his eyes from the blinding lights rotating atop the police cruiser. A firefighter's Nomex gear flashed neon green. I was pinged by a small BB of sorrow when I saw a pair of EMTs guiding a body bag through the front door on a rickety stretcher; we lived in a neighborhood populated by people who would be described kindly as retirees and harshly as geriatric. Only two weeks after we moved in fifteen months ago, Paul Martin, our neighbor to the left, died from a massive stroke; on our right, Todd and Katherine Hummel both used motor scooters and were picked up by a Missouri OATS van to go to the grocery store. Mrs. Gettemeyer, who had to be in her seventies, had creaked up to our door with a tin of stale popcorn and a post-it note with her phone number affixed to the lid to welcome us the day after we moved in, a May scorcher. She and her husband sat on their porch swing most afternoons if the weather wasn't too hot or too cold, and they would wave as Cam and I came and went. Although we lived in the midst of conservative country—during election season, red signs popped up like a plague of bloated, bleeding dandelions—none of our neighbors had batted an eye when I introduced Cam as my partner.

Cam sat down on one of the Adirondack chairs he'd installed on the porch. I sat next to him and took his outstretched hand. He'd helped the Gettemeyers plant hyacinth bulbs in their front yard around a decorative wooden well that one of their grand-children had constructed in a woodworking class he was taking through the continuing education department at the nearby community college as part of his outpatient recovery program from a heroin addiction. Cam's fingers had swelled up in a bizarre allergic reaction, and Mrs. Gettemeyer had rushed about searching through her various medicine cabinets for Benadryl, and then her husband insisted he take Cam to an urgent care center for a steroid injection.

I wondered which of the Gettemeyers was being hauled away by the silent ambulance. Cam started crying, and my heart peeled at his sensitivity. He'd spent years in the NCAA spotlight as a fiery, pugnacious point guard for the Miami Hurricanes before being ousted by a superstar freshman during his senior year; Cam's replacement went on to be a first-round draft pick at the end of the year, while Cam graduated and followed me back to Missouri. Commentators had painted him as an angry kid (he did rack up his share of technical fouls), but I knew that he was actually tender and bendable, easily broken by things like the death of an aging neighbor. I pulled at his t-shirt and lifted him up.

When we moved into our house, Cam surprised me with a reupholstered wing-backed chair and a mahogany side table that he stationed in a corner of our bedroom, calling it a reading nook where I could stack novels to traipse through on cold, rainy days. Although the table was home to a handful of books, the chair was overrun by our discarded jeans and t-shirts, balled-up socks nestled in the corners of the seat cushion. I hadn't sat in it in months. I pulled Cam into the bedroom as the red and blue lights blinkered out in the street, leaving the room shaded with zebra stripes of moonlight.

The ghostly form of Mrs. Gettemeyer was perched atop our mound of loose clothes, a pooled pair of Cam's corduroys like a buoy beneath her.

"Well," I said as Cam sat down on the end of the bed. "I guess that answers that question."

II

Like most people, Mrs. Gettemeyer didn't stay long. She offered Cam and me a quick wave of the hand. We waved back, and then she was gone, wisping into the night like a reflection lost on the surface of a choppy lake. Neither Cam nor I said anything, looking at the swirly spot where she'd been. Eventually our clothing settled back into focus, a pair of running shorts draped over the back of the chair regaining its sharpness.

Cam stared at the chair. I looped an arm over his shoulder and pulled him close. He didn't sniffle or cry or anything, but his body had gone hard as stone, muscles tensed up as if he'd had a seizure.

"Michael Houser," I said.

"Who?" Cam said.

"Your friend Cecelia's boyfriend. He came down to Miami the same weekend I did. We hung out. Went to that frat party where he puked all over the couch while he was dancing on a coffee table. Pretty sure she broke up with him before he left."

"Jesus, Allen."

"What? You got someone better?" I could feel him loosening, his spine unfurling from its cocked position.

Cam sighed. "How in the world do you remember him?"

"He took his shirt off after he vomited. I remember liking his abs."

"God dammit," Cam said.

‡

During the first snow of the year, I was home alone. Cam, an assistant coach for the women's basketball team at SLU, was traveling for a pre-season game against Dayton. A layer of hoarfrost had fallen across our lawn and flowerbeds that morning, a preview of the thick, wet flakes that hoofed down in chunky curtains that afternoon.

At around six-thirty, the doorbell rang. The noise was clunky, heavy; I was convinced that an actual bell was dinging somewhere in the architecture of the vaulted ceiling. When I opened the door, a kid, maybe sixteen, was standing on the porch, propped up by a steel snow shovel.

"Hi." His entire face was blurred by the green of our LED porch light; the past owner had installed it, something about supporting the troops, and because it hadn't gone out, neither Cam nor I had reason to switch it to a normal soft-white, though it did give visitors and deliverymen an alien hue. "Would you like your driveway shoveled?"

"How much?" I said.

The kid shrugged, clusters of acne on his cheeks flashing. "Twenty bucks?"

"Hang on," I said. "Want to make sure I actually have a twenty."

I did, and took his offer. We didn't own a snow shovel, one of those things that it does and does not occur to first-time home owners to purchase and you never remember until after you need it, and then you forget again. The kid threw in the sidewalks free of charge, and for the next forty minutes I listened to him scraping at the concrete, long steady ratchets of noise.

When the bell bing-bonged again, the kid was panting. In the green porchlight, I could see tracks of sweat gathered in the folds of his nostrils, drizzling down his chin like he'd just devoured a peach.

"All done?" I looked past him. "Nice work."

"Thanks," he said, panting. "I'm really tired."

"Don't overdo it," I said.

"You got any Gatorade or anything?"

I told him I could find him a bottle of water. I waved him inside, tromped into the kitchen and pulled one from the fridge. Once I'd delivered it, he ripped the cap off and took a deep glug. I handed him the twenty.

"Thanks," he said, extending his hand for a shake. I took it. "Name's Kevin Douglas. I'll be around."

"Thanks for the shoveling."

"No problem."

I'd have thought nothing of it had the news the next morning not reported that, on the next street over, he'd collapsed of heat exhaustion and died in the hospital.

Which I already knew by then, because only a few hours after ringing my doorbell he showed up at my dining room table.

III

Kevin waved a gloved hand at me and dripped invisible snow onto the hardwood before he vanished. I pressed my toe against the floor after he was gone. The ground was dry.

I went to sleep unsettled. If I hadn't taken him up on his offer, would he have still overheated? What if I'd told him to take off his knit cap and sit down on the couch for a while so he could catch his breath? But what would we have talked about? How would I signal that it was time for him to go?

I said nothing of it when Cam came home two days later.

‡

"How about Frederick Moinahan?" Cam's hands were cradled under his head, arms akimbo. He trimmed his underarm hair with an electric razor, and it was freshly short and fuzzy. I gave his right pit a poke and he spasmed, chuffing out a half-annoyed, half-shocked giggle.

"We talk about Frederick Moinahan all the time."

"We do not."

"We did just three weeks ago."

"Contextualize," Cam said.

"Well, you had just lost when I mentioned Amber Phillips, that girl who got popular after she was hit by a car one day our junior year, and maybe ten minutes later you mentioned Frederick Moinahan, how he threw up during the frog dissection in bio."

"Okay, fine."

Cam had been gone for two straight weekends as the Billikens traveled for conference play. Valentine's Day had come and gone, which really meant nothing to me; we didn't celebrate it, because mid-February was palled by the anniversary of my youngest sister Emmy's death. She was born with progeria, one of those shocking, rare disorders with no cure; this one prevented her from growing up, freezing her body in youth while also rapid-firing her aging process. She'd managed to get to age thirteen, miraculous for someone with her condition, but she suffered strokes, arthritis, and eventually fell into a coma she didn't come out of.

The night of her death, she appeared in my dorm room desk chair. I was nineteen and drunk, having gotten a call about the coma from my mother that afternoon. My roommate had found an upperclassman to buy us a bottle of Popov vodka that we'd mixed with Sunny D. He invited friends into our room, where we crammed on our bunked beds and got hammered, playing Fuck the Dealer and Circle of Death. The room was crinkly and blurred within an hour, and at some point when I tottered off to the communal bathroom my roommate tossed everyone out so I could fall into drunken sleep alone, and when I stumbled back in, there was Emmy, perched on the lip of my desk chair. She waved at me, smiled the healthiest smile she'd ever managed, and then disappeared, the space where she'd been going woozy. I wheeled back out of the room and puked in one of the bathroom stalls, a parade of awful orange. At first, I was sure I'd hallucinated, but a year later, when my grandfather died while I was on spring break, he showed up on my hotel bedspread, his rheumatic fingers twisted in his lap. He unfurled them and offered me a wave just like Emmy's before shimmering away, too.

"It's cold in here," Cam said, knees pressed around my lower ribs. I could feel the cool rub of his testicles against my skin when he bent low to dig at my neck. "You know, after all that heat."

"Mmm." He liked to talk while he worked at the kinks in my back, where my spine was compacted from hunching over a computer all day. We were both slightly broken, him from working with his players, crouched low to demonstrate defensive posture, me from typing. I wrote freelance, working from home in the small office whose window peered into our neighbors' back yard, which was currently piled with another dumping of snow, covering the dormant azaleas and tulip bulbs Cassandra Martin planted every spring. One night a week I taught a creative writing class at the nearby community college because it helped me feel engaged, alive, involved. Cam made jokes about me turning into a lazy sort of writer, the kind who sat around in a bathrobe, drinking coffee and staring outside until inspiration struck. It didn't matter that I didn't own a bathrobe or like the taste of coffee.

Cam ran his fingers through the hair on the back of my head with one hand, the other pushing at the soft wall of my right side. He slid his palm against my belly.

His phone chirped, lighting up the dim room with its technological glow. I left my phone on the kitchen table at night, but Cam couldn't sleep without the world nearby, ever since his younger sister had been in a car accident at two in the morning and his parents couldn't reach him to tell him to hurry to the hospital. It had been serious—she'd suffered deep lacerations to her abdomen and a bad concussion—but she'd made it. Ever since then he'd heard phantom noises of his phone ringing in the kitchen, and I finally told him to just bring the thing to bed.

"It's my mom," he said. I turned over. Neither of Cam's parents ever called—they liked texting, his mother especially fond of bitmojis—and I felt a silvery jolt in my chest.

"Hello?" he said. He put her on speaker. Mrs. Riggs' voice came through crackly, delayed as though she was in outer space.

"Cameron?"

"Yeah, Mom."

"Cameron, it's your dad."

I sprung from the bed, Cam frowning at me but saying nothing. I took a naked lap of the house, pausing in the living room, the dining room, my office. The guest room and basement were both empty. Nothing in the laundry room. By the time I came back to our bedroom, Cam had hung up the phone.

"He's not dead," I said.

"No, he isn't."

"But it's?"

"Not great."

"Well?"

"Heart attack. I told him he'd been grilling too many steaks. It was a doozy, apparently. He'll live if he survives the quadruple bypass."

I could hear the pinch in his voice, that curly high reach that settles in the throat when someone is trying to stop themselves from crying. Cam was crunched up on the end of the bed, and I sat down next to him, curling my arm over his shoulders. His skin was hot, still flushed with sex, but I pressed my fingers into his hair, swishing at the back of his skull. I kissed his throat, just under the jut of his jaw, then slipped around behind him and kneaded at his shoulders. Sometimes, games aren't necessary for declaring a winner.

IV

Cam's parents still lived in their empty-nest nearby; getting to their house took less time on the road than it took for us to get dressed. At her request, we met his mother there rather than at the hospital, where his dad had already been wheeled into surgery. We arrived at nearly one in the morning, bundled in cable-knit sweaters and earmuffs, and Cam nearly wiped out on the driveway, sliding along a patch of black ice the size of a cauldron. His mother was sitting at the kitchen table, an untouched glass of wine and a mess of paperwork in front of her.

"Insurance," she said by way of greeting. "I swear to god this country is fucked."

I couldn't help but smile. Cam demanded his mother step away from the table. She leaned back in her chair and accepted each of our hugs sitting down, and we slid in across from her, Cam mussing her piles and telling her that these technicalities could wait.

"Please," she said, trying to reorient what he'd scrambled up. "If your father doesn't think every duck is in a row when he comes out of anesthesia, he'll just have another heart attack no matter how well they clean out his gutters." She straightened one stack. "How are you boys doing? Sorry for the late-night call."

"We're fine," I said. "How's Phil?"

"Like I said, we'll know more once the doctors open him up." She giggled, and I wondered if the glass of wine before her was the first she'd poured. "Sorry. I'm just imagining your father getting unzipped and *pew*! All his insides come shooting out like a piñata."

Cam smiled, but I could see the tears forming. I reached under the table and squeezed his leg. The only other person he let himself cry around besides me was his mother, who usually opted to ignore his shows of tenderness. She reached for her wine glass, finally, and took a long, three-gulp sip, leaving it nearly empty. When she set it down she stared at it, her whole body swaying just so, as though she was crossing the ocean in a bouncing dinghy.

"I appreciate you boys coming, even though there's not much you can do."

"We thought you shouldn't be alone," I said. Cam's sister was due to fly in at the end of the week, the earliest she could take time off work.

Cam's mom waved away my concern like a pesky swarm of gnats. "I'm not alone. I've got vino and paperwork. What could possibly go wrong?"

We sat in silence while Cam's mother hummed and looked through more tri-folded sheets of thick, embossed paper. Periodically she frowned, or nodded, or shook her head, or took another—this time much tinier and daintier—sip of wine. Sometimes a piece of paper earned a spot on a stack off to the side. Cam and I watched her, he with a narrow, tight diligence, while I tried to surreptitiously look around to make sure I didn't see Phil Riggs suddenly pop up slouched on the ottoman in the living room or leaned up against the dishwasher.

Cam's mother poured herself another glass of wine, offering both of us a helping of the bottle. We declined. Halfway through her drink, she sighed and rubbed her eyes. Her fingers were unpainted, chipped at the distal edges.

We slept in Cam's childhood bedroom, which was still adorned with a bevy of trophies from kiddie basketball. They stared down at us, gloomy and faceless, their burnished surfaces gleaming in the moonlight that dipped in through the window. We groped at each other with a desperate need; I could feel Cam's worry in every touch and kiss; his body's pressure was heavy and leaden, as if his sorrow and concern had turned every muscle fiber into a strand of poured, hardening metal. The bed squeaked underneath us, but Cam didn't care; his mother was out, already sawing snores when we dumped her in her bed, where she had immediately rolled toward the center, arms outstretched into the empty space where her husband belonged.

"Okay," Cam said when we were done. "Umm, Alison Markle."

"Oh, that's a good one." She had worked on the high school newspaper and written a nearly-erotic profile of Cam when he received his scholarship to Miami, a thinly-veiled love letter imploring him to hook up with her. "I've got nothing."

As I shuffled to climb on his back, Cam pressed a hand to my chest. "It's okay, Allen. Not tonight."

"Since when do you not accept the fruits of your victorious labor?"

"Since my dad's in the hospital getting carved open."

I said nothing, instead falling back to the sheets and pulling Cam close. He buried his head in my neck and I felt his warm, doughy breath on my throat, soon joined by the silent roll of his tears.

V

We left for the hospital at ten, Cam's mother's eyes glassy and puffed. But her voice was rich and lively, as though we were headed to a holiday party where she could slosh herself on eggnog and make the other married men feel weird when she stalked the mistletoe, as I'd seen her do more than once while her husband looked on, taking delight in his friends' deer-like fear. She'd gobbled me up in her arms once and kissed me on the cheek, laughing, her rummy breath pungent with star anise as she said she just couldn't bring herself to really plant one on her son's beloved.

My parents, at the end of Emmy's life, spent almost all of their waking hours in the very hospital where Cam's father was laid up, and I always felt the lead of guilt if I didn't go with them. When I would be left alone in our house I would hear all the little noises that homes give off—humming refrigerator, chuffing furnace, settling, moany floorboards and joists—and imagine that they were all groaning at me, embarrassed by my refusal to be at my sister's bedside. So I went, my nostrils filled with the antiseptic smell of the hallways, ears blasted by heart monitors and defibrillators. The children's ward was the worst place to be, full of bald, hollow-eyed pre-teens who looked like they hadn't slept in months. The rooms were all decorated in bright, cheerful colors, the floors and shelves that would otherwise be steel and bare filled with toys and video games and books, anything to distract visitors and patients from the fact that people were dying way before they were supposed to.

Until Emmy died, I only saw the living at hospitals. But then afterward, on the three occasions I'd been to one (first: when I fell out of my bed in my dorm room during a particularly violent nightmare and broke my ankle; second: when my father went in for a biopsy thanks to a strange—and fortunately benign—growth he felt beneath the skin of his armpit; third: when Cam came down with scarlet fever only days after we moved in together), the dead popped up like little flashing ghosts. I knew when someone crashed and didn't come back up; I knew when a cancer patient finally succumbed or a DNR in the gerontological ward slipped away, because they would pop up wherever I was, looking peaceful and prepared, offering me, the only one who could see them besides Cam, a departing wave, like they were on the bow of a ship headed out to sea.

Phil Riggs was in recovery, awake but groggy and unable to sit up or talk due to the fresh sutures on his chest, which were covered in a stack of thick gauze that made him look like an unfinished mummy. Cannulas and IVs swam in and out of his hospital gown, which bowed over him like a glittery shawl. The machinery surrounding his bed purred and bleeped and belched. I felt queasy.

Cam and his mother perched on either side of his bed, blinking at him. Phil tried to speak but all that came out was garbage noise, and Cam's mother shushed him.

"We don't need you to say anything."

When my sister died, my mother wasn't in the room. I was, along with my father. I had backed myself into the corner furthest from Emmy's bed, as if I could burrow into the wall if I pressed my shoulders hard enough. I could hear the flat blare of her heart monitor. There was no dashing rush, no clamor of noise like on *Grey's Anatomy* or *ER* when someone's heart stops. A cavalry of nurses didn't come screeching into the room with a crash cart. No sweaty, suave doctor came sprinting.

We didn't stay with Phil long, but I saw at least two dead people glimmer into existence, one in the visitor's chair next to me, the second right behind Cam. The first was a curly old woman, her back so humped that it looked like her head was trying to emerge from her spinal column. The second was more youthful, a man in his late twenties, with shimmering, shellacked hair. He peered from Cam to me and back before sparking into nothing. The room swam with their departure. Cam's parents were none the wiser, and Cam only seemed to recognize what was happening at the last moment, when he turned toward me and saw the swirly, nauseous space behind him. He frowned in my direction and I shrugged just so. We were, after all, in the hospital.

Death didn't take Cam's father. He was out of it for two days—not entirely unusual, his doctor said; some patients suffered lingering lethargy from the anesthetic and pain meds bashing at their insides—but he slowly emerged from the carapace of his cut-up body, the gregarious smile crowning his face once again. Cam's dad was an insurance salesman who had somehow made what I'd always thought of as a dregs-of-the-sales-world job into something lucrative; their house was all expensive crown molding and flashy electronics and steel appliances. He was capable of charming the most curmudgeonly prospective clients. His laughter sounded like Santa Claus offering up good tidings at Christmas. When he was released from the hospital into the care of Cam's mom, who was burdened with a list of doctor's orders about as thick as a Dickens novel in one hand and a sack full of prescription medications in the other, he waved at the nurses and doctors while Cam wheeled him to the elevator bay like he was a beauty queen leading a parade.

‡

A week later, after Cam won a game of Forgotten Folk by bringing up a member of our high school marching band who showed up to the Homecoming parade drunk and sprayed his fellow trumpet players with vomit when he lost his cookies during the school fight song, we were interrupted by the sudden appearance of Todd Hummel, our aging neighbor on the right. He sat where Mrs. Gettemeyer had appeared, on the edge of the wingback chair. Cam didn't see, his face smashed into a pillow—I'm pretty sure he'd fallen asleep—so it was only me who gave him a wave goodbye. Mr. Hummel smiled, revealing a toothless, gummy mouth, and then vanished off to wherever he and the rest of our ghosts went.

VI

I thought sometimes about what it would be like to see Cam go. Somehow, I'd become convinced I would outlast him despite his better overall physical fitness, his smarter eating habits, his better family history—Phil's bypass excepted—when it came to heart disease, cholesterol, and high blood pressure. I tried to imagine where he would show up, what he would look like as a dilapidated old man, still kind and glowing even if he was weathered and bent. And, of course, what I would say to him in that dazzling last moment.

But whatever forces run the world had other plans. I was only thirty-six when I started suffering explosive migraines like ice picks were being buried in my skull above my right eye. Other symptoms came: flashes of horrible light. Nausea. Memory problems. I was hit with, most terrifying of all, periods of aphasia, words clinging to my skull but refusing to come out of my mouth. When my doctor came into the exam room with the results of my battery of tests—blood, lymph, spinal tap, CAT scan, MRI—I could see the words in his mouth before he opened his lips.

The tumor was malignant, and I dripped and drizzled away in a haze of pain medicine. Exploratory surgery confirmed that it was too huge and gangly, reaching out into the folds and gyri that made me who I was, for extraction to be an option. I spent hours tilting through nausea following intense chemotherapy and radiation. Cam bought me marijuana from a kid some of his basketball players knew at SLU, which took some of the edge off and gave me something of an appetite; I could stomach wheat toast with a small pat of butter. Cam leapt to the toaster the minute I had it in me to eat.

I didn't see another dead person after my diagnosis. All of our parents were still around, even Phil Riggs, who had lost a ton of weight when he switched his diet to kale smoothies and vegan burgers that he glumly blinked at as he cooked them on his five burner grill, pretending they were his favorite sirloins and baby back ribs. Everyone walked around me on tip-toes, pretending to ignore that my hair was falling out, my eyes were sunken, my back curved with atrophy. I tried to make jokes about my exhaustion and decay; I couldn't even sit at my computer long enough to type up a paragraph, so I laid on the couch and dictated to Cam, but only for an hour at a time because he would start crying.

Sex was no longer on the table; my bevy of medications came with horrific side effects, including erectile dysfunction. We still played Forgotten Folk. Cam still kissed my now-sunken chest from time to time, his lips silky like rose petals, but he would cry as he held onto me at night. I lost control of my memory. I know I repeated names, but he never said a word. He always let me win, though he could hardly give me back massages because the lightest touch would hurt, and I couldn't lie on my stomach without feeling like I was about to vomit.

"What about Jolly Farberger?" I said once. Jolly had been my best friend in high school, a football star smacked down by an ACL tear when he went to Michigan.

"You may be sick," Cam said, "but you know neither of us has forgotten Jolly Farberger."

I was in the hospital. Cam visited every day, even though I told him he didn't need to. I could feel it coming, the end: I could hardly see straight anymore, and the word *palliative* had slipped out of more than one doctor's mouth. I barely ate. I lived in a bubbly haze from the morphine drip sluicing into my veins. Sometimes, I thought I could see the dead again, bodies showing up in blurry flashes at the end of my bed, but that was usually just a night nurse or one of my parents or Cam, watching me and, in the latter case, trying and failing not to cry.

Cam was in the bathroom when my final moment came; I could hear his urine hitting the sharp inner curve of the wide, squat toilet with its grab bar. I didn't call out for him or groan. A corkscrew feeling jammed into my navel, and my throat closed. If there was any pain, I didn't feel it.

I did manage to wait, to perch on the edge of the bed, feeling amorphous like loosed water, and it took every last bit of my will not to dissipate like mist before Cam finished washing his hands. When he stepped out of the bathroom he saw me, and though I wanted to say goodbye, all I could do was wave. He cried out and tried to rush to me, but in a heated flash I vanished, gathered into a bright, demanding warmth before everything blinkered out. I was calmed and comforted, though, knowing that as long as Cam was around, I would not be forgotten.

HEAVE YOUR DEAD TO THE GROUND

Hearts fell first. Harvey watched as they landed in yards, pelted shingles, dented the roofs of mini vans. They destroyed gardens, squashed slicing tomatoes, bruised spinach leaves. They knocked branches from trees and smeared blood on bay and picture and double-hung windows, left dark streaks on doors, on driveways, on sidewalks, on patios. They stained Harvey's freshly-sealed deck and frightened his dog. They frightened the neighborhood children, they frightened him. They filled the air with slapping noise and knocked over mailboxes. They bloodied skylights. They sat on driveways, shriveled like dead jellyfish, like deflated kickballs, like slabs of sallow meat. Harvey knew people ate chicken hearts, lamb hearts, cow hearts, ate them grilled and baked and stewed and stir-fried. He'd heard of beef heart stew, beef heart kabobs, pork sorpotel and bopis, pan-fried chicken hearts, pate with hidden heart, chicken heart stroganoff.

But these were human hearts.

"What the hell is happening?" Lawrence said, calling from Palo Alto. He'd been offered a one-year visiting professorship and had taken it. He and Harvey were trying to make it work.

"I don't know. What are they saying on the news?"

"You haven't watched?"

Harvey shook his head, then remembered Lawrence wasn't there. "I've been looking outside. The hearts are everywhere."

"What do they look like?"

Harvey speared open his blinds. His house sat on the main thoroughfare that wended through his subdivision.

"Like fists," he said. "Like fists with all the blood gathered in the knuckles."

"How are you feeling about it?" Lawrence said.

"What kind of question is that?" Harvey said.

‡

Harvey watched professionals in hazmat suits bend over the hearts, scooping them into biohazard coolers while men in tweed carrying shiny, leather-covered bibles screamed about the Rapture. Newscasters stood on sidewalks, their cameramen more concerned with where their feet fell than with getting a good shot in the right light.

An email appeared in Harvey's inbox, inviting him to the home of the president of the HOA. When Harvey knocked, the president looked nonplussed by the hearts dotting his yard like large, lumpy dog turds. He waved for Harvey to come inside, where he offered Harvey a beer. The rest of his neighbors were drinking buttery white wine and standing in the kitchen around the island.

"So what do we think this is about?" someone said.

"Am I dreaming? Are we all dreaming?"

"Well, wake me up. I hate this."

The president calmed the screamers down as he refilled glasses of gewürztraminer and whisked away empty St. Pauli Girls. Even though he was wearing a t-shirt and chinos, he moved like he was wearing a tux and waltzing. He had long black hair that curled around his ears and shone in the pendant lights descending from the ceiling. Harvey looked away, but nodded when the president took his empty beer bottle and asked if he wanted another.

"Who here is driving, right?" the president said with a wink.

When he came back, beers slick with condensation, he told everyone he'd already called the city.

"What about our yards? Our driveways?"

"How much will it cost to get cleaned up?"

"Are the hearts toxic?"

The president raised his hands, palms facing outward. With lidded eyes, as if he was in a trance, he said not to worry. He would make some more calls. The word *calls* was like a lullaby.

"When I walked outside, I'd almost forgotten about the hearts," Harvey told Lawrence on the phone that night.

"Sounds like you're in love."

"Whatever. It's weird shit."

"Weird shit brings people together."

"Lawrence."

"I'm tired."

"It's not even ten there."

"Long day tomorrow. Meetings. I'm gonna let you go."

As Harvey set down his phone, he thought of the moment that afternoon as he picked his way down the street. He'd glanced back and seen the president standing on his porch, smiling and nodding, as if to say, "Yes, go, yes, you can make it home. Everything will be alright."

‡

Eyes, looking like desiccated grapes, fell next. Most burst into iridescent goop, but a few retained their shape, bouncing off the soft surfaces of plastic playhouses, buoyed by creeks, pillowed by piled leaves. They stared up, wide and unblinking. Optic nerves fluttered like torn feathers.

"I swear," Harvey said, "one of the ones that fell in the front bushes looked like my grandmother's. I'd recognize that shade of blue anywhere."

"Lots of people have the same color eyes," Lawrence said.

"Okay. Sure. Fine. I know that."

More body parts fell. Intestines left brown trails behind. Livers landed with sickening sex-slaps against front stoops and bedroom windows. Harvey watched jawbones stick in yards like thrown horseshoes, teeth looking ready to chatter out terrifying hymns. He watched ribcages come crashing into the street, bones splintering into strewn hay. Spinal cords clattered against sliding doors, tangled themselves in wicker furniture. Stomachs trapped themselves in pergolas, bloaty with acid that ripped through paint and primer and wood and metal and sucked the life out of flowers and grass.

Harvey received another email invitation to the president's house, but when he showed up, he was the only person there.

"Hi," the president said. He had a pleasant baritone. He stepped aside and gestured for Harvey to come in.

"Am I early? Late?"

The president laughed. "I thought we could think it out one-on-one."

"Oh."

Beers were already waiting, sweaty Schlafly hefeweizens sitting on the kitchen island. The president popped them open and handed one to Harvey. After he drank, he said, "They're all unreasonable. Convinced the world is coming to an end."

"They could be right," Harvey said.

The president laughed. "I guess they could be. But they have kids or grandkids to worry about. It warps how they see things."

"I'd say what's happening is pretty warped," Harvey said.

"Oh, I know." The president set down his beer and leaned against the marble so his triceps flexed. He was wearing a snug blue Under Armour t-shirt.

"What did you think you and I might figure out that the scientists haven't?"

The president smiled and shrugged. "What are your theories?"

"I don't really have any."

"You haven't dreamt or thought about it or talked it out with anyone?" The president drank. "What do your friends say?"

"My friends?"

"Surely they have opinions."

Harvey bit his cheek. How to admit to the president that he'd moved here for Lawrence's graduate program at Wash U, that he hadn't seen his friends in ages, that the only person to whom he had any connection was now halfway across the country?

He was saved by the hands. Their sudden arrival was hard and loud. Harvey and the president rushed to the living room window to watch them fall. The fingers landed in a vast array, some clenched into fists, others splayed like they were about to be buffed at a nail salon. Some broke, skewing at unnatural angles. Others pointed to the sky or poked into soft soil. They curved into letters in American Sign Language. They caught in the crepe myrtle in the president's yard and the planetrees and hedges across the street. The sound of them hitting sedans and tool sheds was like the end of the world.

‡

People arrived in droves. They took pictures. They set up food trucks. Men and women with bullhorns preached the gospels while their followers swayed, hands up and eyes closed, their voices shattering the morning quiet while Harvey slept. He pierced his window blinds, and groaned, seeing clumps of people up and down the street, eyes rolled toward heaven, hands clasped. He wondered if he could call the police and complain about noise.

Harvey watched them stare at the sky. He opened his front door so he could hear, and felt a hard anger when he heard one man ask God for more body parts to fall. They picked through abandoned yards for dried-up pancreas and testicles and tarsal bones left behind by the scientists, shoving them, without fear of contamination or illness, into plastic containers and paper bags, as if collecting icons of departed saints. He watched them scrape up humerus bones from sidewalks using snow shovels. They collected blood dripping from trees with vials and buckets and pitchers you might use to serve beer.

I saw you on the national news, Lawrence texted. A reporter had caught Harvey in his driveway while he was checking the mail, dodging around a fresh rain of toes. They reminded him of maggots, and he'd stepped on one. It had let out an unsatisfying, wet crunch. The reporter had not asked him much, sticking a microphone in his face and asking for a quick sound bite while his camera operator stared at the sidewalk once he'd gotten Harvey in-frame. Harvey hemmed and hawed, blinked and squinted into the sun, and couldn't even remember afterward what he'd said.

A few families moved out, tried to sell their houses unsuccessfully, took out second mortgages so they could rent apartments somewhere else, where roofs weren't subject to flapping, heavy lungs. They pulled their kids from their Montessori schools and private Christian academies to save on tuition. Images of houses, close-ups of yards and trees drizzled with viscera while preachers and gawkers and lab technicians bristled on the sidewalks, appeared online. In the pictures, yards were weedy. Bushes were unkempt, tangled with blood vessels. Harvey watched the neighborhood go to seed, turning into a series of haunted houses, full of whispers and dust and ghosts.

"Have you heard the conspiracy theories?" Lawrence said.

"Conspiracy theories?"

Lawrence told him: people thought it was all an invention, that all the photos and videos were doctored. That Harvey and his neighbors were attention-seekers living boring lives in the suburbs who hated their jobs as bank managers and primary school teachers and IT specialists and low pay-grade accountants.

"Jesus. Of course we're not making it up."

"Some say that the government is running experiments and are dumping their refuse from the tippy-top of Earth's atmosphere," Lawrence said.

"You don't believe any of that, do you?"

"Then there's the theory that the parts aren't real. Plastic and corn starch and rubber."

"Lawrence," Harvey said. "You know it's all real, right? I've seen it up close."

"But you're on the inside," Lawrence said.

"Ha." Harvey knew Lawrence was joking. Or, at least, he thought so. He felt a spike in his side. You could never be sure, could you?

"You could come out here," Lawrence said.

"And do what?"

"It was just a suggestion."

Harvey said nothing. Neither did Lawrence. Though they were both breathing, it was as if they'd hung up.

‡

Two emails arrived in a row: a third invitation to the president's house, a follow-up meeting and barbecue, the language fluffy and enthusiastic, as if the world wasn't falling down around their driveways and front stoops and raised-bed gardens. Then a note sent only to Harvey promising that this time it would not be just the two of them.

"I hope," the note ended, "that you didn't feel deceived last time."

Harvey didn't respond, but he did go.

The president served stuffed olives and hard alcohol. He smoked ribs and Harvey could smell them as he walked up the driveway. Inside, everything sparkled and the air was filled with Pledge, PineSol, apples and cinnamon. Harvey stood around, drinking from the rum and coke he'd been poured, and listened to everyone complain. Eventually he made his way onto the back patio where the meat had curled into hard, dark slabs. The president was alone out there.

"I'm glad you came," he said.

"Thanks for having us."

"I feel like it calms them down."

"The olives are good."

The president smiled. "You can thank Trader Joe's, then. I just paid for them."

"An important step."

The gathering passed into evening. More people arrived, and most of them got drunk. They stumbled away after filling their bellies with the ribs, which were tender and spicy. Paper plates were scattered across the kitchen island. Harvey started stacking them, pulling plastic forks and shredded napkins into their own heaps.

"No need," the president said.

"Just trying to help," Harvey said.

"Oh, you did," the president said. He was rinsing off a pair of tongs. He turned from the sink. "Just by being here."

Harvey felt like he'd swallowed a jawbreaker, a hard ball of steel hanging in his throat.

‡

"People here have theories too," Lawrence said. He'd called late, nearly eleven. Harvey's eyes were heavy. He could still feel the pulse of rum in his limbs.

"I bet they do."

"Do you want to hear the wildest?"

"Do I?"

"One woman said to me, 'Maybe heaven is kicking out its dead.' How lame is that?"

"We don't really have any answers."

"I didn't say you did."

"No, you didn't."

"You should come out here. Just for, like, a week."

"I'm really busy," Harvey said.

"Doing what?"

That night, Harvey dreamt he stood in heaven on its pillows of cumulus. He could see the blue-and-brown marbled earth. God stood next to him, heaving bodies toward the continental

US. Harvey watched them break apart upon entry into the atmosphere, blood and bone and viscera spreading in an atomized cloud. He woke sweaty. He wiped his brow and squinted in the dark to make sure he wasn't oozing blood.

‡

Phalanges were little hailstones on skylights. Latissimus dorsi muscles flailed down like fallen stingrays. Harvey sent the HOA president a picture. He responded with a landscape of his back yard covered in mammary glands.

The crowds had thinned, whether out of impatience, an overload of grotesquery, or something else, Harvey wasn't sure. Scientists still milled about, ready to collect fresh samples, but most of them had packed up, trundling off to labs to study the body parts. Harvey had no idea what conclusions they might draw. Reporters had stopped coming around, realizing the story wasn't developing into anything of new interest aside from the question of the day: what would fall next?

"Things are feeling quieter," Harvey said to Lawrence.

"You sure you're not just acclimating?"

"I know my own experience."

The president called, and Harvey answered, his mouth sticky before he even said hello. Without any hesitation, the president invited Harvey to go for a beer.

"Somewhere that we won't have to worry about falling body parts."

"I could do that," Harvey said.

They sat on the patio at what the president called his favorite bar. Their table, wrought iron, was shaded by an umbrella advertising Michelob Ultra. The president ordered them a pitcher of his favorite pale ale. They squeezed orange slices into their pint glasses.

"I think it's going to stop soon," the president said.

"You do?"

"I've been keeping track." He told Harvey how he'd printed off lists of the various human body systems. "Did you know we have eleven of them?" He listed them off. "We mostly only think about the musculoskeletal, because it's what we can see the most." The president flexed his bicep, which bulged beneath the roll of his sleeve. He laughed at himself and drank. They fell into a long silence.

"You like it here?" the president said finally.

"I grew up in the suburbs. Chicago."

"So it's all familiar."

"I stayed there for school." Harvey almost started in on his entire story, how he and Lawrence met at Northwestern, Harvey graduating with a degree in English not because he wanted to write but because he loved nothing as much as he loved reading books. How he'd followed Lawrence, who had been accepted into the Brown School of Public Health and was now doing a stint out in California. How Harvey loved the job he had at a cozy bookstore, not just selling novels but working the books—he'd minored in accounting, for no reason other than the pride he took in his math skills. But the president didn't ask, so Harvey didn't share.

"This is nice," the president said. He waved his hands toward the parking lot and strip mall around them. "No ears falling upon us."

"It's weird how easy it is to talk about it."

The president drank. He smiled. "Things happen that way sometimes."

The air was tinged with that far-off smell of coming cold. Harvey thought of wood fires and fallen leaves, even though the only sign of change were the first, briefest streaks of ochre in the trees. He thought of winter festivals, light shows, walking along lit paths while holding a hot chocolate spiked with Rumplemintz, arm threaded through Lawrence's pea coat.

"Do you think we'll ever go back to normal?" he said.

"I don't care for normal." The president refilled his beer, asked Harvey if they should order another pitcher. When Harvey nodded, the president said, "Normal is boring. I like things that are different."

"So this is all okay for you then."

The president shrugged. "What is okay? Okay can become good or bad quick, you know?"

Harvey blinked and looked toward the sky, his gaze so intense the president twisted to look, too, but there was nothing to see.

‡

"They're offering me another year," Lawrence said.

"Already?"

"Should I take it?"

"How can I be the one to answer that?"

Harvey had taken to pacing the house when they talked on the phone. He glanced outside. The house across the street was empty. Ulnar bones had slashed through the trees in the night.

"I want to know what you think."

Harvey was thinking about his body, his self. After they'd finished their second pitcher, the president drove them home, stopping outside Harvey's house, his F-150 growling as it idled on the curb. Before Harvey got out, the president touched his hand. Harvey thought they might kiss, but instead the president said, "Let's do this again. It's nice to get out."

"Yeah," Harvey had said. "It is."

How, Harvey thought, would anything seem whole again when he'd been subjected to the show of so many disparate parts? At night, he trembled as he imagined the fallen hearts and hands and eyes. The lightest whuff of noise jolted him, sent him rushing to a window to check for cheekbones bashing at the glass.

Lawrence sighed. "Please," he said, voice strained like a bowstring. "Just tell me what you're thinking."

"I don't know what I think. I think you have to choose."

"Will you come be with me?"

"What about the house?"

"I have an apartment. There's plenty of room."

"We have a lot here."

"There's a lot worth getting away from."

Harvey sucked in a breath. "I think it might be ending."

"How can you know that?"

Harvey's still-living heart fluttered, capillaries squeezing blood to the surface. He shut his still-living eyes. His still-living hands were clenched, his calves tight.

"Sometimes," Harvey said, "I think you just know."

FOR RENT

The artist living in Valerie's ribcage would like to know if she could please try to tone it down with the rough sex.

The thing is, Val tries to explain, Jace is the first boyfriend she's ever had with visible abs, and well-manicured pubic hair, and leg muscles whose striations she can see twitch when they move, so she feels like stifling their loose rollicking might be asking a bit much. He's also funny and smart and sensitive and after they make love he holds her in his arms and she feels enveloped in clouds.

Sighing, the artist runs a hand through his hair, which is always shining and slick like he's just showered, though she's pretty sure he hasn't found a way to install a bathroom in there between her intercostal muscles, but everything in that region is numb now anyway, so who can say. It's like breathing while buried in snow.

"Okay," he says, nodding. "I get it. I like abs, too. Who doesn't."

He wonders, though, if she could try to keep her window of vigorous love making a little more, what's the word, consistent.

But that's the thing, she tells him. It's the *spontaneity* that really gets her going.

He says he knows. The way her heart starts thumping is like someone banging on a steel bass drum right next to his easel. It sounds, he says, like the world is coming to an end.

‡

Val loves her job. She's the leasing office manager for a three-story mixed commercial/residential building across the street from an uppity liberal arts college that is all cherry trees and brick and white wainscoting. The first floor of the building contains a Turkish hookah bar, a bookstore that competes with the one on campus, a florist shop run by a tiny Italian man who smells like wet dog and greets her with sloppy kisses to each cheek when she visits, and, soon, a bakery/bar specializing in petit fours and margaritas, the lease just signed yesterday by a couple perhaps three, maybe four years older than Val. They held hands even as they scribbled their signatures on the thick pack of papers.

Val's main responsibility is filling the vacant units on the upper two floors, twenty-four in total, which is no trouble at all. The humanities kids across the street froth at the mouth for the loft spaces with their exposed duct work, fifteen foot ceilings, chocolate-colored concrete flooring. It makes them feel bohemian, hip, and they string Christmas lights along the mother-of-pearl walls and line the tiny balconies with tomato plants. A stack of crinkled and coffee-stained rental applications teeters on her desk, unread. If a unit opens up, someone inevitably walks in the front door looking to fill it, and she takes the keys and shows off the apartment, lease signed that day.

Jace, who teaches economics at the college, appears in the office with a bouquet of roses bought from the Italian man next door. He is wearing tight jeans and a button-down shirt with nothing underneath, revealing a triangle of browned skin beneath his throat. Val sets the roses down and puts up a sign in the window saying she's showing a unit and will return shortly, then she locks the door and drags him to the back, tugging at Jace's belt buckle. He stumbles behind her, jeans falling to his ankles. He takes her from behind, and she willingly presses herself up against the wall. She pulls at his collar, bringing his chin over her shoulder, and she makes her voice raspy like a chain-smoking rock singer and calls him Dr. Aubuchon, saying it over and over as he thrusts, and as she whispers she can feel him tensing up inside her, his body stiffening, and he comes faster than usual, groaning, his breath milky and warm like the heat from an oven, and the flow of his air over her ear makes her tremble too, her legs squeezing together as she gasps.

On his way out, she knows she'll hear it from the artist, but she just shrugs and smells the roses, goes looking for something to put them in, front and center on her desk, so every stranger she sees will know she is loved.

‡

The device is situated just below her left breast. When the artist first attached it, cheeks red and fingers wobbly as he tried to avoid copping a feel, it didn't so much hurt as pinch and expose, the little clamp digging into her skin like a cat kneading with its claws. The diameter of a silver dollar, the plastic caster looks like the end of a tube of toothpaste, circular with a half-inch nozzle poking out. A third nipple almost, Jace said the first time he saw it after peeling off her shirt. He caressed it, and she grabbed his hand and moved it around her body to her bra strap.

When Jace bounces out of bed in the morning to go for a three-mile jog before his macro class at ten, Val flicks the cap open and out comes the artist like a genie freed from its lamp. His gassy-liquid body makes a slurping noise like a kid eating spaghetti, and he materializes in a blur, gradually pixelating and becoming real. The artist is slouching and thin. She's sure he doesn't have abs. There's no where to do crunches or wind sprints in her ribcage, in the first place.

She browns him toast and brews Darjeeling tea because she thinks that's the kind of thing an artist living in a ribcage would want, plus he never objects, sitting at her breakfast nook and slumping over the plate, crumbs dotting the white porcelain like scattering stars. She lets him use her bathroom when he's done, and she listens to the sound of his urine hitting the bowl. When he comes out, he wonders again about the love making, but with a wry smile, like he knows he needs to say something but that it will do no good. Then he nods, and Val unbuttons her shirt, flaring it open on either side so her belly is exposed, and she pops open the device and he is sucked back in, offering a little wave of his spindly artist hand before he evaporates into her chest.

‡

Before the artist moved in she was living in her parents' basement, sleeping on a daybed whose lumpy mattress felt like it had rat skulls sewn into it. Val had graduated from college with a degree in history. Intending to become a high school teacher, she quit her internship after three days, the ammoniac smell of teenage boys making her ill, the dead-eyed glare of gussied up girls turning her insides to ash. She finished her coursework to calm her parents, but she slunk back to them, jobless and alone, unpacking her bags in their basement that smelled like a fish tank. She shared their master suite because the showerhead in the guest bathroom was broken, sending sprays of water across the tile floor. When she brushed her teeth, she shared counter space with her mother's Aqua Net and her father's minoxidil foam. She accepted a job bagging groceries. Her uniform was canvas blue, like a painter's smock, two sizes too big.

One day, on her way out the door and smelling like stale donuts, she saw the sign posted on the cork board, among business cards for traffic attorneys and realtors and babysitters: an artist, seeking residence. The pay was staggering, written in sharp black lines. Valerie ripped the whole sign down so no one else could take the little pre-cut tabs bearing his phone number, not thinking about the fact that he'd probably posted flyers in every grocery store in town.

No matter: she called him that afternoon, and very suddenly was no longer alone.

‡

She thinks: Well, it was bound to happen. Law of averages will catch up with you, of course. At first, as Valerie tried to angle the pregnancy test so she peed on it and not her hand, she'd been terrified by the prospect. Three weeks late, the notion of a child budding in her uterus: she'd trudged to the too-bright CVS, with its buzzing lights and piano music squeaking out the loudspeakers and periodic interruptions from the pharmacy calling some tech back from a smoke break, and stared at the wall of pregnancy tests, their rainbow of colorful boxes boasting faster, earlier, clearer results. Images of sticks with blue lines, baby faces, words printed in slanted, Victorian letters. She'd plucked off one from eye level, told the aging cashier she didn't need a bag. Paid by credit card.

And now here she is, the message clear as day: preggers, a little cluster of cells seething below her belly button. She and Jace don't use condoms because she doesn't like the feel of them, the barred, caging friction of interruption as they link themselves together. But Val has popped birth control pills like clockwork, a little chirping alarm on her phone reminding her at lunch every day to reach into her bag and extract the little pink button. Perhaps the blame belongs to the glass of red wine she and Jace drink each night? Could that get in the way? She should ask her OB/GYN, but first she'd have to find an OB/GYN. She doesn't know where to find one. Maybe the artist knows. He seemed to know so much, even though he lives in such a small space.

She wonders how he'll feel about a roommate.

‡

Jace proposes during a romantic dinner at an Italian restaurant, tea candles casting shadows along his sharp jaw that is dotted with a well-manicured, week-old beard. His Adam's apple is a delicate point of darkness. The linguini is thick and buoyant, and the smell of his steak makes her salivate and want to vomit at the same time. Six weeks of such splitting dualisms: she is horny and nauseous at once, suppressing the need to upchuck into the trashcan next to her bed while also seething with satisfied relief when Jace enters her and moves with slow care. He's afraid of hurting the baby, and she tells him, the first time, that it's a good thing he's an econ teacher because he'd be terrible at biology because there's nothing he could possibly do to their child.

He kneels down on the scratchy carpeted floor after their waiter offers dessert, which Val waves off without a second's pause. The box is blue velvet like something plucked out of the Indian Ocean, the ring inside pearlescent and slim. It fits perfectly over her knuckles, nestling against the fatty rib of her hand like an anchor. At the table next to them, a white-haired couple watches the proceedings and offers a cozy round of applause when Jace stands and embraces Val. The couple tip their wine glasses toward Val and Jace, the woman's eyes crowding with tears. She reaches for her husband's hand and their droopy flesh kneads together, and when Jace offers his lips to Val for a kiss, she wants to swallow him, too, hold the entire world that she loves inside her belly.

‡

She tells the artist during one of their breakfasts, leaning back in her chair, hands magnetized to her stomach, left hand cradling the cleft beneath the hard bulge, right cinching around the knob of her belly button, fingers fiddling and coaxing it like a loose ring. The artist's expression doesn't change, the gait of his chewing on the slightly-burnt toast uninterrupted. His hair is longer, curling around his ears in bushy tufts. It sweeps across his forehead like thin bird feathers.

He swallows and washes down with a slurp of tea, then sets down his mug.

Val has moved into Jace's three-bedroom condo. Fifth floor of a seven story building, speedy elevator that smells like cinnamon.

They've assembled a crib, picked out a soft green for the walls, bought a rocking chair and changing station at IKEA. In the open-concept living room/kitchen/dining zone, the artist looks out of place, a funeral dirge during karaoke night.

"I know," he says. "About the baby. Already."

"You know. How."

"I could tell. I feel him kick at night."

"Him?"

"It's a him."

"You can't possibly know that. How would you know that? I didn't know that. We wanted to be surprised."

The artist apologizes. Says maybe he's wrong. "But congratulations. I'm happy for you." His voice is matted, flimsy. He looks exhausted, Val realizes. His eyes like raccoons', skin drooping, wrinkles crowding the corners of his mouth.

She shakes her head, changes the direction of the conversation, tripping over the words like they are Spanish. She tells him they're starting a family now, and things are different.

He stands, and flicks his fingers toward her with a snap of his wrist, a mixture of dismissal and disgust and understanding, all balled up in one motion. He gets it. He understands.

"It was bound to happen," he says. "I told you."

She wants to say that he never told her. The artist never said anything of the sort. In fact, he said so little, munching on his toast, squawking about her sex life, taking a tiny bit of her breath every time he splashed out of her body. Yet he was so warm. Even though she was numb there where he sat tucked away inside her body, she could always feel him squirming around. She could feel when he was painting, a faint tickle near her sternum, a hiccup in her pulse. Since the baby's conception, it's been a symphonic echo around her heart like the boom in your chest after hearing the smash of a bass drum.

But she says nothing, just uncorks the plastic cap and watches him fizzle and fade, stoppered back into her body, another settled mass.

‡

The mishap occurs during her seventh month. At least the lights are off, the soft fuzz of the moon outlining their bodies. She and Jace are nude from the waist down, sex no longer the prowling, intoxicated drizzle of passion and pleasure but a functional relief for the pressure in her groin. Val's feet are swollen and she craves Diet Pepsi and scrambled eggs at all hours, which Jace dutifully retrieves, stocking their fridge with enough dairy and soft drinks to feed a dozen. They're spooning, his knees pressed against the backs of her legs, and they rock gently like they're in a rowboat, his hands around her waist. At some point he shifts and loses his grip, his hand flicking and pushing the cap open with a light pop. Val, so focused on the relief—and tamping down the rising need to pee—doesn't notice the artist appear until Jace yells out, pulls himself from her, and covers them both with the kicked-off blanket that has gathered like a snowbank at the bottom of the bed.

"What the fuck," he says, and Val realizes she's never heard him yell before. They've never fought. She thinks, for a moment, that it must be a sign, but she's not sure if it's a good or a bad one.

"What's going on?" The artist's voice is as bleary as he is, shimmery, a half-ghost in the darkness.

She can sense the tension radiating off Jace. An exhaustion hits her, all parts of her spilling open, and she caps and uncaps the device so that the artist barely has time to congeal into a real person before he's pulled back in, his voice wobbly like he's yelling from under water, but she can't understand a thing he says. He may be screaming, he may be laughing. She shuts her eyes, ignoring Jace's shifting weight, and barely has time to lock the artist inside before she falls asleep.

‡

On the artist's last day, Val slips her oafish body out of bed early, Jace stirring in his half-sleep. She waddles to the kitchen and lays out the lavish spread she's planned: twin bouquets of baby's breath and carnations, one on either side of the table, on which she places plates full of warm bursting sausage, a wheel of mozzarella cheese, petit fours from the bakery, kept fresh and cool in the refrigerator, sugary white squares that look like toys out of a child's play kitchen. Heaps of fruit whose juice gathers on the porcelain in a pinkish pool. Large glasses of milk and a pot of artisanal tea, the sharp, bitter smell like wet earth flopping her stomach. The baby kicks toward her ribs like he's riding a bicycle.

But when the artist emerges, he looks at what she's done and sighs. "You shouldn't have. I'm really not hungry." When he sees the pinch of disappointment that Val can't help but let seep into her face, he reaches out and plucks up a grape. She can hear it pop against his cheek when he bites into it.

Propped against his feet, hugged to his body so she can only see the off-white backing, is a heavy-looking canvas.

"I have a gift for you," he tells her. Then he hefts it up and spins the painting around.

It takes Val a moment to absorb what she's looking at: a massive, reddish eye, swirly and just so blurry. The rusty color of a brick wall, the eye is streaky but lifelike, the lines of the eyelid detailed, pupil on the verge of dilation.

"It's yours," the artist says. "It's your eye."

"What did you paint it with?" Val asks. "It doesn't look like normal paint."

The artist's face lightens, and he grabs another grape, gnashing on it and swallowing before he tells her: it's made of you.

He explains: he has drawn her blood and bone, bits of muscle that he's scraped away from inside of her, all ground down and mixed together and put on the canvas. The eye is made, he says, of hundreds of tiny images of her. When she leans close, she sees it: tiny versions of herself, meticulous and exact, head and shoulders, her chin turned down toward her right shoulder, eyelids shut, hair wafting in an invisible breeze. Though small, they are as detailed as the eye itself, each one just slightly different: an alteration in the angle of her face, the curl of her neck, the square of her shoulder.

Val shuts her eyes. The nickel scent of her own blood brings a bilious wave up her throat.

"Each day," he says, "I painted you after breakfast."

"I don't know what to say," she manages. "It's beautiful."

Which is true. But what is also true, what she doesn't say, is that she hates it. That her body has been excavated, her disparate parts moshed together to make this bloodied mess whose color reminds her of an uncooked steak.

The artist leaves unceremoniously, slipping out the door before she has time to process his sudden absence. When Val sets the painting against a table leg and rushes out after him, the hallway is empty. She considers taking the elevator down, seeking him out, but she knows she will never find him. A certainty settles in her chest that he has disappeared forever.

She also knows she cannot show Jace the painting, that he'll dismiss it as grotesque and inappropriate, so she hides it away in the back of the closet behind her shoes, the eye facing the wall. What Val doesn't know is that she'll put the painting out of mind until, three years from now, when she is pregnant again, she'll run across it as she cleans out the closet when she and Jace are moving out to a suburban ranch house, and her body will clench up when she turns the canvas and finds the eye staring at her. Their son will toddle to her and screech and want to know what the picture is, and before she gives it a second thought she will drag the canvas out to the garbage chute in the hallway and throw it down. She will not know yet that her pregnancy is ectopic, the baby lodged in her fallopian tube, and that the embryo will have to be excised by laparoscopic surgery. Nor will she see that the artist's portrait will become stuck in the chute when she chucks it down, hovering for days until dislodged by a trash bag full of beer bottles and rotting cabbage when it finally crashes into the garbage bin, slicked with the seepage and leak of strangers' wet refuse.

‡

Labor should be simple, but Val does not want to let go. In spite of the twists of pain as her body contracts and works to expel her baby, Val fights against the emptying feeling creeping from her spine. She's numb below, but she refuses to let her body cooperate, her doctor becoming frustrated and red-faced, snarling at her from behind his papery surgical mask that she has to push. Finally, sweaty and dislodged, Val complies. When the baby finally crowns and slips out like a dropped sock, she is overcome by the emptiness of her body. Like a deflating balloon she wilts, and even when her little boy is placed in her arms still gooey-haired, limbs flailing in jerky movement, his weight pressed to her chest, she continues to seep away. Jace grips her shoulder and smiles down at mother and son, and Val tries to muster the gumption to return his grin, but she feels like there is nothing left in her body to offer.

‡

She brings the baby to the office, and on the days he doesn't teach, Jace joins them. Instead of quickies in the back, they eat lunch together, Jace armed with roast beef paninis wrapped tight in shiny tin foil. They chew in quiet and the baby gurgles. All of the residential units upstairs are full, so there's never anywhere else for Val to go.

One day, a prospective renter for the last empty commercial unit comes in. Val swallows her bite of sandwich and leaves Jace to watch the baby while she presents the space. The walls are in need of drywall and paint, and the floor's cement is like that of an unfinished basement, chalky and white with dusty grit. As the man considering the space blusters about potential layouts for his office—he's looking to start up his own law practice, thinks he can make a killing helping minors from the college out of alcohol possession tickets—Val takes a slow lap of the space, breathing in the wet, untouched smell. The room is barren, but she can feel its cloying possibility. She runs a hand over the hard space between her breasts. Tickles her fingers across the keys of her ribcage, whose feeling has reemerged, a hard warmth.

The man nods and says he think this will do, screw it, I'll take it, let's do it.

Val drums her fingers along her body, the echo buzzing against her clenched teeth. She lays her hands along her once again flat stomach, and finally comes to rest on the asterisk-shaped scar where she removed the artist's clamp. The skin is raised like Braille, but when she presses her fingers across she can read nothing in the bumpy ridge. Val wonders how one gets this way, taut and slim and emanating body heat while still craving to be filled again, ever tipped and ever hungry.

I WILL EAT YOU, DRINK YOU, I WILL BE FULL

Michael swallows his ex-boyfriend in one huge gulp. Dustin showed up an hour after Michael sent him the break-up text, pounding on Michael's apartment door. At first, Michael was afraid that Dustin's fists would punch through the flimsy wood and then bash his nose to smithereens like he'd nearly done a few weeks ago, barely missing Michael's nostril and instead starfishing his cheek with deep bruises. It had been Dustin's first outburst of physical violence, and it left Michael with a long headache and a pulsing in his jaw that no amount of ibuprofen or pressure with a melty icepack could make go away. In the aftermath of the punch, Dustin wept, apologetic and gooey. He draped his body over Michael's where he lay prone on the couch and sobbed into Michael's shoulder, begging forgiveness that Michael was quick to give with a short bleep of "Okay, okay," followed by pats on Dustin's back.

As Dustin continued to knock, Michael shivered and felt ghostly pain in his zygomatic bone and was about to rush toward his bedroom, but then he decided: no, it will not go like that. So Michael took a deep breath, opened the door, and plucked Dustin into his mouth before he could get a word out. The last thing Michael saw of Dustin was the cherry-red of surprise on his face when he realized what was happening.

Dustin goes down smooth except for his Birkenstocks, which lodge in Michael's throat in a Naugahyde clog. Michael uncaps a bottle of water and drinks it in four hearty swallows. He loosens a leathery belch and feels Dustin settle into his stomach with a soft *kerplunk*, like a stone being dropped into a pond. Michael leaves the empty water bottle on his kitchen counter among his dirty plates and crusted cereal bowls. His messiness is a thing that drove Dustin to fits, who insisted on emptying trash cans when they were barely half-full and always wanted to wash out beer cans as soon as they were cashed, crumpling them down for recycling immediately with his thick, powerful fists. Dustin bitched about the flecks of hair Michael left behind in his bathroom sink after he shaved, and God forbid there be the slightest remnants of spittle on the mirror from his spazzy electric toothbrush.

"But it's my bathroom, not yours," Michael made the mistake of saying once. "Why do you care how clean it is?" Dustin replied by stomping into Michael's kitchen and grabbing up a roll of paper towels and throwing them at Michael's head.

"Alright, alright," Michael said, wiping away at the marble until not one stray hair was to be found. When he was done, Dustin investigated, then, standing behind Michael, threw his arms around Michael and gave him a tight hug, whispering, "See, isn't this so much better?" before nibbling on Michael's ear, his breath warm like melted wax.

To celebrate the consumption of his ex, Michael makes a mess of his apartment. He unfurls the afghans he normally drapes over the back of his couch and sends magazines spraying across his coffee table. He enters his bedroom and pulls the t-shirts and boxers that poke out from his bureau's drawers and scatters them on the floor. Then he lies down atop his twisted sheets and pulls up the hem of his t-shirt. Michael tinks his fingers against his ribs, then slaps at his abs, humming.

"Hope you're comfortable in there," he says. Michael looks at the clock on his nightstand. "Uh oh. If I don't leave now, I might be late for work." At this possibility of a failure of punctuality, Dustin squirms in Michael's gut. They once slipped into a play—community theatre, for goodness sake—thirty seconds into the show, and all night Michael could feel Dustin fuming. He didn't even clap when the curtain fell, even though the production of *You Can't Take It With You* had been quite funny. The car ride home was silent until Dustin pulled up to Michael's building and said, "Maybe I should sleep at my own place tonight." He left Michael standing on the curb, blinking, and didn't call or message him for two days, until he showed up with Chinese food, which Dustin knew made Michael gassy.

‡

They met at a party Michael threw during his junior year of college. He'd managed to snag a low-rent one-bedroom above a busy Chinese buffet, inexpensive mostly because it was pungent with the miasma of used fryer oil, which sat in a large disposal contraption in the alley behind the restaurant, the smell wafting up toward Michael's window, which he had to keep open in the hot months because the window A/C unit was fritzy. Michael drowned the odor with so much air freshener that the apartment took on a foggy haze.

The air was just going crisp with chill. Michael and Dustin were introduced early in the evening, Dustin charming with his dimples and short-cropped hair and straight nose, with his deep voice and white cable-knit sweater that managed to show off the sculpt of his shoulders and the heave of his biceps. But then Michael didn't see or talk to him until much later, after the entire party made an exodus, half of them to go home, the other half to trudge off to some other rager they'd heard about. Michael thought he was alone, but then he heard the flush of his toilet and Dustin stepped out of his bathroom.

"I think they forgot you," Michael said.

Dustin let out a half-yawn, half-belch, and stretched, arms lifting high enough to pull up his sweater to reveal a tight slab of stomach. "Are you hungry?" he said. "I'm starving."

Michael's refrigerator was pathetically understocked, mostly crammed with half-empty cases of beer people had brought to the party, along with a dying gallon of milk and some eggs that had probably oxidized. He found a jar of creamy peanut butter on top of the fridge and pulled out a pair of spoons from his utensil drawer. Dustin seemed satisfied with this offering, and they sat side-by-side on the couch, the peanut butter on Michael's coffee table between them, where it sat nestled between half-empty plastic cups and discarded beer cans. They took turns dipping their spoons into the mouth of the jar, saying little. Eventually, Dustin accidentally smeared peanut butter on his upper lip, and before he could stop himself, Michael reached out and whisked it onto his pointer finger. He froze, finger in Dustin's face. They stared at one another, and then Dustin smiled and licked the peanut butter off, taking the tip of Michael's finger in between his lips. Michael's whole body went hot and stiff. After several seconds passed, Dustin set down his spoon. As Michael took his hand back, Dustin pounced, leaning over and pushing himself atop Michael and kissing him hard on the mouth, his breath buttery and thick.

In the morning, he helped Michael clean. Dustin wandered around the apartment in only his boxer shorts, and Michael stared at the long leanness of his body as Dustin plucked up cans and emptied flat mixed drinks down the sink. Michael liked the way Dustin's feet shuffled across the carpet and how his lats stretched when he leaned down to grab up garbage. Dustin whistled, then hummed and smiled. He kissed Michael before he left, his tongue and teeth fuzzy with sleep, but his breath sweet. He pressed his hand against Michael's chest and said, "I left my number on the kitchen counter." Michael found it tucked under a three-quarters full bottle of wine Dustin had re-corked. He called the next afternoon, and Dustin answered.

‡

Michael falls into a light, sweaty sleep, from which he is ripped by a burning, bilious sensation in his throat. He runs to the bathroom, stubs his toe on the door frame. His hand catches on the light switch. He doesn't have time to make it to the toilet, to toss open the lid, before a waving pulse echoes up his throat. He vomits into the sink.

It is not sludge. It isn't acid or gunk or dry heaves.

It's Dustin.

But it's also not Dustin.

He is gooey, his clothes a seeping wreck. Michael blinks at him, cankered into the sink. Dustin's shirt and pants are too big on him; his neck is narrower, his shoulders have lost their breadth. His hair is floppy and long, shellacked by the glue of Michael's esophagus. Michael recognizes this version of Dustin. He's seen him in photographs in Dustin's high school yearbook. This is pre-college Dustin, seventeen and string-beaned.

"What the fuck," teenage Dustin says, wriggling from the sink and looking down at himself. "What the fuck did you do?"

It wasn't until college that Dustin started lifting weights and swallowing down shakes made chalky with grainy protein powders, drawing out the muscle that Michael knows so intimately, the quads he's run his fingers over, the arms that have smacked at him and threatened hard fists. But this Dustin is still pissed, screaming and yelling and cursing, moving toward Michael, who backs up against the towel rack.

"Calm down," Michael says.

"Fuck no I won't calm down," Dustin says. He's drippy and slimy, but this makes him more frightening.

So Michael eats him again.

Dustin, prepared, resists a little, pushing his boy-fists against Michael's chest as he grabs him. But these noodly muscles of Dustin's don't pack their usual punch. His fingers press against Michael's cheeks, ballooning them out, but down he goes. Dustin shrieks, his voice echoing in Michael's throat, and his shoes—the same Birkenstock numbers—are just as chewy and thick. But Dustin splashes down anyway, and Michael, sweating, leans against the bathroom sink, taking deep breaths. He looks at himself in the mirror, hair askew, eyes bleary with tears. He turns on the water and splashes his face, cups his hands and drinks. This Dustin isn't quite as filling; Michael feels some space in his gut, and so he goes to the kitchen and scrounges for food. He fries an egg in his skillet, sunny side up, then swallows it down in two bites. He cooks another egg and feels the yolk break on his tongue, coating his mouth in its gooey richness of cholesterol. Then he eats another. That's plenty, he tells himself, but then he fries a fourth, and, feeling a sense of fullness, toddles back to his bed and lies down, letting the gurgling noises of Dustin settling carry him back to sleep.

‡

Four weeks into their relationship, Dustin, lying next to Michael, their legs a tangled heap of patella and tibia, said, "I have to make a confession."

"Oh jeez," Michael said. He rubbed his eyes. "Should I be worried?"

"I don't know."

Michael sat up. "Now I'm scared."

"You're my first boyfriend," Dustin said.

"What?" Michael looked down at him. Dustin's shoulders were turned in, like he was a bug trying to curl into a tiny heap.

"What I said. You're the first."

"That—that doesn't make sense," Michael said. He remembered how assertive Dustin had been their first night together, falling atop Michael, his breath a mix of beer and peanut butter, sour and salt. The press of his lips, hard and knowing. His hands, moving across Michael's stomach and into his jeans without a blip of hesitation.

"You were so sure of yourself," Michael said.

Dustin stared at the popcorn ceiling. "Not really."

"You fooled me, that's for sure."

"I could never tell anyone."

Michael leaned up, weight on his left elbow. "What do you mean?"

Dustin shook his head, eyes flashing in the dark like little strobes. "I couldn't tell my parents. My mom still doesn't know." His father left when Dustin was fourteen. "But I think my sister suspects."

"Do other people know?"

"My friends. They're not stupid."

Michael leaned down and kissed Dustin, a light peck on the side of his mouth. His lips were the smooth underside of a flower. "How am I, so far, for a first go?"

Dustin, eyes closed, nodded. "You're perfect."

‡

At work, Dustin sloshes around while Michael builds submarine sandwiches on artisanal bread at a local shop known for its home-made mustard. Michael ignores the woozy feeling he gets when Teenage Dustin's hand punches at his gut's wall. He wills his body to up the strength of its stomach acid; picturing Dustin's skin melting away so all that's left is a bunch of click-clacky bones helps ease his upset.

He drops a muffuletta on the floor and relishes in the splattered mess of meat and the swishy puddle of olives and oil and vinegar. Before standing back up, he slides his index finger around on the floor and moves it toward his mouth; Dustin lurches in his intestines and Michael lets out a silent laugh, then washes his hands, muttering joyously to himself. His customers, men and women in business attire rushing from one meeting to another, mostly smile and say thank you, though a few frown and tap their feet while they wait for their meatball subs. Others bark into cell phones, mixing angry exhortations with their requests for the spicy mayonnaise or for Michael to go light on the spinach mix. Some of them tip, dropping bills and coins into the carafe stationed next to the cash register, and Michael calls out thanks as those generous customers leave. He pats at his stomach every time he says the word *you*.

When the lunch rush recedes and Michael starts to pound dough for a fresh pan of house-baked rye, he almost forgets that Dustin's even in there. He normally takes a short break to eat his own sandwich, but he's full, full, full. He can't imagine he'll ever need to eat again.

‡

Shortly after he and Dustin started dating, Michael found himself plagued with an insatiable hunger; his stomach was forever growling, and he gorged himself on granola bars, pizza, scrambled eggs. It must have been all the exercise he did with Dustin, his metabolism thrown into a high-geared tizzy by the morning runs Dustin dragged him on, the trips to the gym for leg-busting squats and deadlifts, chest-frying bench presses and arm-noodling Zottman curls and pullups. But at the time he wondered if his nutrients and minerals were being sucked out by a parasite, a tapeworm lounging in his intestinal loop. He ate and ate, Dustin watching him polish off heaping helpings of lo mein or mashed potatoes or pasta primavera. Michael ordered three, sometimes four, drive-thru cheeseburgers, or an extra handful of chicken wings at their favorite dive bar. Dustin chirped and shook his head, but no matter what Michael ate, he never felt full.

‡

Michael skips breakfast. When he drinks a glass of water, he can feel it sit high in his stomach, threatening to gurgle up and choke him. He tries doing some pushups, which go alright, his pectorals filling with the warm heaviness of blood and lactic acid. Michael imagines Dustin's fingers pressing there, just below his collarbone, telling Michael he has to elevate his feet if he wants to isolate the top half of the muscle. When he tries crunches, he feels like his bowels are going to slip open. Teenage Dustin didn't yank Michael from sleep during the night, but now

Michael feels the same disruptive gurgle, the growing nausea. He hikes himself to his feet and rushes to the bathroom. He flings open the shower curtain and heaves into the tub, his jaw achy, his throat billowing.

This Dustin is even stickier than the last, but he's smaller: ten years old, give or take a year. The clothes are ridiculous, the t-shirt like a poncho blistered by heavy rain. In adult-Dustin's shoes, kid-Dustin looks like a boy clomping around in his father's loafers. The jeans slide right down his hips, taking the plastered underwear with them.

"Oh jeez," Michael says, looking away. "Here." He throws Dustin a towel.

"What's the matter?" Dustin says, his voice trilly and scant, yet just as angry as Michael remembers. "You knew this would happen."

"I just needed you to calm down."

"Bullshit. This is such bullshit, Michael. You're such bullshit, you know that?"

For as fast as Michael's heart is beating, and despite the gruesome smell coming off Dustin—he reeks like days-old food left out in the hot sun—Michael can't help but laugh at the diminutive voice trying to sound big and tough. It's like the one time Michael and his friends huffed helium in high school, sucking it out of balloons they bought at the grocery store. They sat around thinking of the dirtiest things they could say in Mickey Mouse voices, leaving themselves hunched over and laughing at their own absurdity.

"Stop yelling, Dustin," Michael says. "You always yell."

It's the wrong thing to say. Kid-Dustin balls his fists. He frowns, a scarlet sheen vibrating from his cheeks, clear and hard despite the goopiness of his skin.

"You fucker," Dustin says, stepping out of the tub. Dustin, his body suddenly lacking coordination, trips on the lip of the bath, one of his now-too-big shoes catching on the edge, and he trips. Michael reaches out to stop him from slamming his face on the linoleum, but Dustin is slick and he slides right out of Michael's grip, his hands squeaking along the floor. He starts howling wordless rage.

If Michael weren't unnerved, he might sigh. Instead, without saying a thing, he plucks Dustin up and swallows him for the third time.

‡

One night, Michael sat on Dustin's bedroom floor, leafing through the yearbook Dustin kept on his nightstand beneath his alarm clock.

"As a reminder of who I was," Dustin said. He didn't let Michael look at it at first, but he finally gave in. "If it'll get you to stop asking."

Michael gathered up the various images of his boyfriend as a teenager, gangly and slim. He was on the basketball team—"a benchwarmer"—and the jersey threatened to slip off his coat hanger shoulders in the team photo.

"Come on," Dustin said eventually, tweaking Michael's shoulder with his fingers. "Let's get some sleep."

"I'm almost done," Michael said. He was poring over the senior page Dustin's mother had bought him. The images were of a Dustin that Michael didn't quite know, a kid with glasses—he'd switched to contact lenses the summer before college—and t-shirts a size too large and ears that looked cartoonish with his hair cut short.

"You're so different now," Michael said.

"Yeah, well. Aren't we all."

"Am I?" Michael said. He poked at his own arm; thanks to their trips to the college gym three times a week for the last several months, he didn't feel as slack as he used to. His midsection was truncated with more muscle than it used to be, the area around his bellybutton a swirl of ravioli-shaped lines. When he touched his own knee, little threads of muscle blossomed in the periphery.

He shut the yearbook and slid it beneath the clock.

"Satisfied now?" Dustin said.

"Yes," Michael said, hoping the uncertainty in his voice wasn't as plain to Dustin as it felt.

‡

Michael stumbles through sandwich orders in a daze. He forgets the extra cheese on a tuna melt, then squirts mustard instead of mayo on a turkey sub. The owner, a sixty-something named Ted whose white hair is buzzed short and has rosacea-glowing cheeks, raises an eyebrow and tells him, after Michael takes his first break, to go home and rest. Michael tries shaking his head and is about to say he's okay when Ted raises his hand and says, "I'll pay you for the rest of your hours. But you're sweating on my cold cuts."

Michael is dizzy when he gets home and he's barely able to make it up the steps to his apartment without toppling over; he grips the railing hard, flakes of rust from the old iron smearing against his palms. Kid-Dustin has spent the last four hours throwing a horrible prepubescent tantrum. Where his larger iterations didn't have the space to move around and do so much damage, this younger Dustin is beating on Michael's insides like his organs are a drum set. Michael can barely breathe when one of Dustin's feet manages to gouge its way up at just the right angle, catching the lower reaches of his lungs.

Dustin throws himself into his bathroom, on his knees in front of his toilet. For once, he's glad Dustin insisted he clean it the weekend before, when Michael whisked the brush around the porcelain, scuffing away all the moldy refuse caught on the inner lip; the water smells like alien-blue cleaner when he puts his face over it and tries to puke. He sticks his fingers in his mouth; they taste of the plastic gloves he wears when building sandwiches. He presses at his gut with his free hand, poking at the tender space below his belly button. Michael lays his palm flat on his lower abdomen, his pinky finger grazing his crotch, and he can just about feel kid-Dustin swimming around in there in his intestine, sloughing along the velvety tissue of his duodenum and jejunum. He pictures Dustin, eyes smeared shut, as he wobbles through, being crunched upon by bacteria.

And then Michael throws up again.

This time, Dustin's feet are too small to have brought along his shoes. Michael coughs and dry heaves and when they're finally out he tosses the soaked Birkenstocks in the tub.

"You're such a prick," comes a child's voice, five-year-old Dustin with bleachy hair and blue eyes that are too big for his face. He windmills his hands toward Michael, who leans back and collapses against the tub taking heavy, wheezy breaths. Dustin's little feet kick and splash at the toilet bowl's small puddle of water, his heels squealing when they slip against the porcelain (his socks are still somewhere mucking in Michael's digestive track).

"You know," Michael says between gasps. "Maybe if you'd stop being so nasty to me, I wouldn't have to keep doing this."

This gives little Dustin pause. He cocks his head, a quizzical look on his face. "Nasty?"

"You're kidding."

"I'm never nasty. Criticism isn't nasty, Michael."

"Good lord," Michael says. He leans up, back onto his knees. They ache against the hard flooring. "You don't get it, do you? Why do you think I broke up with you?"

Before little Dustin can respond, Michael grabs him by the fleshy back of his neck like he's nabbing a kitten and swallows him down.

‡

"I think," Dustin said, "that I might love you."

They were sitting on the floor in Michael's living room, playing Monopoly. The overhead light was turned off, and they read the properties and counted their money by the light of three

LED candles Michael had perched on the coffee table. They were celebrating their three-month anniversary.

Michael, who had just landed on Saint James Place, cleared his throat and passed Dustin—playing banker—the one hundred eighty dollars to buy it.

"You think?"

Dustin smiled. "I think." He passed Michael the property card, and their fingers touched.

"Such certainty you have."

"Well, it's hard to be sure."

"Why's that?"

Dustin looked down at the board and picked up the dice. They were sitting cross-legged, and Dustin's jeans were pulled tight against his thighs. "Because I don't think I've actually been in love before."

"First time for everything," Michael said.

Dustin rolled. He, too, landed on Saint James Place. He picked up a ten and a five and held them out.

Michael smiled and told Dustin to keep his money. "For being brave," he said, and leaned over the board, angling his face toward Dustin's, their chins illuminated by the plastic candles and their glowing light.

‡

Five-year-old Dustin doesn't stay down long. Michael's body heaves, recognizing something dangerous and painful. His breathing shallows and his stomach contracts and he barely has time to stand up before he's back on his knees, his innards thrumming. He can feel the plumb weight of Dustin as he erupts back up his throat. He keeps his eyes closed as he listens to the plunk of Dustin falling out through his lips. Michael's body feels wrecked; he isn't in pain so much as emptied out. He opens his eyes, and there, of course, is a tiny, infant-sized Dustin, swaddled in the twisted, ropey fabric of his shirt, the green gone forested dark.

This Dustin does not scream. He doesn't threaten with clenched fists and teeth. Instead he cries, squalling out indiscriminate noise. Michael reaches out a trembling hand and tries to soothe, wicking one finger against the slick baby-Dustin's cheek; his fingernail digs a rivulet of gunk off Dustin's face.

"It's okay to cry," Michael says. "You're confused and angry and sad. I know the feeling."

Baby-Dustin shuts up and blinks at Michael. His eyes are a sharp, Arctic blue.

"It's hard to imagine you ever being this small," Michael says. He grips one of Dustin's fatty arms, all the bone and muscle dissolved into a chewy goo. "How did you start this way?"

Dustin gurgles, his eyes rolling, head lolling like his neck is a Slinky. His fine, translucent hairs are smeared in a swirly cowlick. His arm is so tiny and breakable in Michael's hand.

"I'm sorry I did this to you," Michael says. "But what choice did you give me?" He hears, in that moment, something like Dustin in his voice, an edge elbowing its way to the forefront.

His plan had been to eat him again. To slurp Dustin down, hopefully for the last time, because what else was there for Dustin to become? The steady erasure of his years would lead to a blinkering out, a simple vanishing from the earth. But now, a better idea.

Michael takes Dustin from the toilet. He starts kicking and squalling immediately, but Michael ignores the tantrum and wraps him up in a towel, taking the time to wipe him down, remove as much goo as he can. Then he swaddles Dustin up tight, like he's wrapping a gift.

They only went to Dustin's hometown once, a quick drive-by, but Michael thinks he remembers the way; two hours, a straight shot down interstate 70, past Columbia. He'll have to guess at the right exit, but he can picture the gas station with its red portico on the frontage road where they filled up, Dustin buying a pair of bloodred slushy drinks for them while Michael worked the gas cap on Dustin's car. He remembers the little subdivision, the squat ranch house in between larger Victorians. He'll find it.

"Please stay still," he says, setting Baby-Dustin on the passenger's seat of his car, tightening the seatbelt over his little body. "I'm not trying to hurt you."

He pays attention to the road; his hands grip the steering wheel so tight the top layer of leather flakes off on his hands. Michael's blood pounds in his ear. He feels like he's going to throw up, but there's nothing in him to expel. Baby-Dustin lets out gurgles of resistance but falls asleep during the first ten miles. Michael doesn't bother with the radio.

He finds the house; he remembers the hydrangeas that line the front porch and the pots of Bob Marleys hanging from the awning. And the door: painted a seafoam green, a little burst of Oceania in middle America.

A car is in the driveway. No matter. He gets out, careful to make minimal noise closing the door, and picks up Dustin from the seat, silently begging him not to cry.

"I'm sorry, Dustin." He pokes a finger toward Dustin's mouth. His baby lips grab at it like a fish nibbling for food; Dustin's saliva is warm, his mouth gentle, soft. As Michael walks up the driveway and then the path leading to the front stoop, he keeps talking at a low whisper. "I don't think I wanted to destroy you. Just change you."

He reaches the porch. Michael leans down and sets the baby on a bristly welcome mat, trying to be careful so the harsh material doesn't catch the back of Dustin's head.

"But there's no changing you, I know." He looks down. Baby-Dustin blinks at him. "But maybe you can start over."

Then Michael rings the doorbell. Before he can reconsider, he rushes across the grass to his car and scrambles in. He turns the ignition. He doesn't look to see if someone answers the door. As he drives away, his gut roils with the engine. He's thirsty, and that familiar, unassailable hunger is back.

LOOK AT ME

Doug Pfluger was pretty sure he was not a vampire. He loved his mother's pesto, which was loaded with freshly-crushed garlic, and he stared at himself in the bathroom mirror smeary with crusted spearmint toothpaste every morning to poke, prod, brush, and comb his unruly cowlick, and he sat on the spongey lounge chairs next to the pool in his back yard on the weekends, soaking up the sun while the neighbor dog barked and ran the length of the cedar-planked fence. When he let his mother and father drag him to church on Sundays the holy water didn't burn his fingers or forehead. And yet the morning after he made out with Trey Bonomo in Trey's Honda Accord, Trey called, wanting to know why the sun was hurting his eyes and blistering his hands so badly.

"And my cat keeps hissing at me."

"And I really want a bloody steak."

"Oh, and I have no reflection. My hair looks awful. I think."

Doug examined his teeth in the mirror, pulling back his lips to expose his gum line. He pressed a thumb against one of his canines, which didn't look or feel any longer or sharper than usual. He opened the door to his parents' bedroom, where a cross hung over their bed, bejeweled and lacquered, the edges a dark onyx, and when he hopped up on the giving, squeaky mattress he had no problem touching his palm to the cool metal and felt no burn, no achy unpleasantness. He slept through the night just fine, waking at the honk of his alarm as always.

He found Trey leaning against his locker. Even though it was mid-September—the weather was still pungent warm so the air smelled like a swamp—Trey wore heavy layers, a long-sleeve shirt covering veiny biceps, a scarf wrapped around his throat like a coiled snake. A pair of leather gloves sheathed the hands that had dashed across Doug's jaw the weekend prior and a baseball cap tilted over Trey's forehead. The bits of his face Doug could see—Trey's nose, his chin, his cheekbones—were blistered and blasted like Trey had been slapped over and over.

"I told you, something's wrong. The sun hurts."

Trey's skin was usually a warm bronze, the color of fresh caramel; he spent hours on the tennis court over the summer, shirtless, working on his backhand and serve, lathering himself to a sweat doing footwork drills and sharpening his volleys. Doug was his hitting partner, not on the team but popping balls over the net for Trey and spending those hot hours watching the twist of Trey's muscles, which were lean but refined, his legs particularly striated already, teardrops of quad muscle gathered around his knees.

"Oh," Doug said, and before he could stop himself he reached out and pressed his fingers to Trey's reddened skin. Trey jerked back, eyes wide, and looked around the bustling hallway.

No one knew about them. They had been careful, telling their parents they were going to parties or to the movies with clusters of their friends when they were in fact alone, sometimes at a small Mexican restaurant a town over where the refried beans leaked small lakes of grease and whose sodas tasted flat, other times sitting on the squeaky pleather benches of a shoe store in a mostly-abandoned strip mall where no one bothered them and they held hands and stared at the hundred-dollar Air Jordans. On weekend afternoons, sitting in the mall ten miles north, they shared jumbo pretzels caked in too much salt. They dipped them in neon orange cheese. Trey always drove because Doug didn't have his license yet, not because he was too young, but because he hadn't tried to pass the test, unsure of his ability to parallel park or remember when to look over his shoulder. Trey would settle his Accord two blocks from Doug's house and they would sit in the thrummy, warm night, the interior of the car illuminated an evil lime green from the dashboard and radio displays and they would lean into one another, Doug inhaling the arctic scent of Trey's deodorant while he worried about his own breath and body odor, convinced, despite Trey's assurances that he smelled pleasantly of almonds and fresh bread, that he was cadaverous and tainted like an abscess.

"I'm sorry," Doug said, pulling his hand back as a gross of cheerleaders rushed by, lips sparkling glossy pink. "No one saw."

"I can't sleep at night," Trey said. "Ever since."

Trey's hand hovered near his neck, and Doug remembered: he'd been lost in Trey's skin. Before he'd thought about what he was doing he was kissing Trey's throat, and then it wasn't just a kiss but a small nibble—or what he'd thought was small, but was apparently much larger, because Trey had jerked back, squeaking out a pained noise, and slapped his hand to where Doug had, without realizing it, taken out a small square of flesh.

Trey's eyes were bloodshot, as if he'd been smoking weed with the stoners behind the auditorium before school, a cluster of stoop-shouldered boys—and one girl, hair dyed seafoam green—that even the principal had given up on, resigned to the illegal inhalations happening on the property. Word was that he'd struck a deal with them: smoke all you like as long as you don't reek of it in class and you pass biology. The stoners had one-upped him, dousing themselves in beauteous colognes and perfumes and acing their exams, publishing operatic letters in the school newspaper about equal rights and the importance of a free press. Doug once had a crush on one of them, a tall, brooding kid with broad shoulders that looked wide as eagle wings in his black t-shirt. His eyes were lined with mascara, but this somehow gave his face a delicate depth, accenting the sharpness of his jaw and the striking slimness of his nose.

"I don't know what to say," Doug said as the bell rang and students began scampering into nearby classrooms, the halls emptying like a tub whose drain stopper has just been yanked.

Trey shook his head, adjusted his baseball cap, and shrugged his shoulders, jouncing the strap of his backpack slung against his back.

"Do you want to hit today?" Doug tried, his voice straining.

"I don't know if I can. My eyes and skin."

Doug swallowed. "Okay." He watched Trey turn and walk away toward his math class, regretting that he hadn't reached out to squeeze Trey's gloved hand or brushed his fingers against his neck buried in the silky scarf.

Doug skipped first hour history, partly because Mrs. Grakowski didn't take attendance and just showed old movies about World War II. He sat down in the library, the woman at the circulation desk eyeing him over her coke-bottle glasses but saying nothing when he opened up his English textbook and appeared to be studying. He was really looking through his cell phone, exploring WebMD and doctor.com, trying to diagnose Trey. Doug himself didn't feel any different than usual aside from the sparkled high that being with Trey—even seeing him ill, or whatever he should call Trey's condition—left punching at his arms and chest. A saline warmth permeated his body when they touched, as if part of Trey was melting into Doug, leaving him tingling and aware and sharp, as if the lines of his body and face were otherwise blurry and wishy-washy and Trey's touch gave him definition and meaning. This feeling always lasted, pushing through him like he imagined the rush of cocaine or speed would.

He found nothing online, and when the bell announcing the end of first period buzzed through the quiet library, he spasmed in surprise—a chalky smirk flashed across the librarian's face—and rushed to shove his book into his bag and stumbled off to chemistry, where Trey was his lab partner. This was his favorite class of the day, when he could be near Trey without anyone feeling out a sniff of what was going on between them. They could lean their heads together over the balance scale, touch one another's wrists while pouring acid from bottles, and pretend it was out of precaution and safety instead of tender want for physical contact.

But Trey wasn't there, his stool a jarring empty space next to Doug, who couldn't follow Mrs. Wizell's lecture on balancing equations. He didn't even write down the homework assignment when class was over.

He did not see Trey again that day. Doug snuck text messages, his phone jammed against his crotch in English and trig while he typed blindly, staring up at lessons on sine and cosine, even answering a question about *Catcher in the Rye* while his thumbs danced across his screen's surface. Trey did not respond. Doug felt an uncoiling in his stomach like his innards were a snake slowly waking and stretching, biting at his stomach lining and squeezing his heart.

But Trey did appear that night, rapping on Doug's window while Doug sat at his desk, reading through his Spanish textbook. The noise startled him, so jarring he almost fell out of his chair, and when he turned to the window he had to stop himself from screeching. Trey was perched on the sill, one hand clutching the window frame, the other knotted in a fist.

Doug's bedroom was on the second floor, and his window wasn't near any ledge or jutting part of the roof.

"I can fly," Trey said when Doug opened the window. Through the screen came the hazy buzz of insects. "And look at this."

Trey smiled, and there they were: a pair of fangs, teeth oversized and cartoonish, glistening with Trey's spit.

"I can smell your blood. The scent is stronger when your heart beats faster. You're warm." He winked.

Trey looked better, his skin back to its normal smooth bronze, like that of the tiny shimmering bodies on soccer and basketball trophies. His eyes were glossed white, pupils narrow even though it was dark outside. He'd ditched the accoutrements, and his thick black hair wavered in the night breeze.

Doug shivered. The word *warm* coming from Trey's lips was seductive and thick.

Trey tapped the mesh between them. "Can you open the screen?"

Doug pried at the plunger bolts holding the tension springs in place and managed to pop the screen open while Trey hung from the window, the toes of his shoes pressed lightly against the narrow strip of wood jutting out like a thick lower lip. Doug pushed the screen wide enough that Trey could slip into the room.

"You'll have to invite me in."

"Okay. Come in."

Trey swooped through like a gymnast and planted himself on the end of Doug's bed. Doug pulled the screen shut again and then locked his already-closed door.

"Just in case. My parents."

"I know."

Doug wasn't sure what to do with himself, so he stood by the door. His heart was thumping fast, so hard he was sure Trey could hear it. His breathing was shallow, as if he'd just finished a series of wind sprints; he felt ragged inside, torn and ripped. They'd had sleepovers when they were kids, of course, Trey sprawled out atop a slick, ribby sleeping bag that Doug's mother would root out from the cluttered basement, but this was different. The air was damp, thick with teenage musk, that cloying, acidic odor that follows adolescent boys around no matter how much showering or deodorizing they put themselves through, a miasma filled with Taco Bell and farts.

"You don't have to be scared of me," Trey said. He flashed his teeth, parting his lips and poking the tip of his tongue against his fangs. "After all, you did this to me."

"I don't really get that."

"You must have. It's okay." Trey shrugged. He was wearing his letterman jacket; on most people Doug thought they looked cartoonish, puffy and one size too big, even for the linebackers whose swagger had only grown after they won the state championship last season, but Trey's fit him perfectly, creasing over his shoulders and arms in a way that made him seem larger than life, a bursting giant. He slipped it off, revealing a ribbed sleeveless t-shirt, the kind Doug knew Trey knew Doug liked on him. Trey licked his lips. "Now that I've figured it out, it's kind of great."

He patted Doug's bed. Doug felt himself move across the room and sit next to him.

"Want me to show you?"

Trey's breath smelled of cashews and yeast. Doug felt the brew hall smell pass over his skin, the little hairs on his neck standing at attention as Trey fit his mouth against Doug's throat.

Doug leaned away.

"What's wrong?" Trey said. Up close, Trey's pupils shined like oil slicks.

Doug sighed. "I don't know. This feels strange."

Trey laid his hand on Doug's thigh and pressed his fingertips against Doug's quad muscle, kneading at his skin. "Just relax."

There was an edge in Trey's voice, one note off-key: not anger but a grunted-out want for control, a fuzzy spangle of frustration.

"I just—well, I like sunlight. And garlic."

Trey rolled his eyes and stood.

"Fine," he said. "Just think about it, okay?"

And then he was gone, out the window in a flash, so quick that Doug didn't have a chance to tell Trey he'd left behind his jacket. Before Doug pulled the window closed, he looked out into the night, listening to the soft wash of breeze as it rattled the maple trees in the front yard. He imagined Trey bounding through the dark, soaking in the blackness and the silver of the moon, his arms wide open as he embraced his new sordid self, the one that Doug had, inexplicably, created.

‡

Trey stopped showing up for school, and tennis practice was out of the question. He did appear at Doug's window most nights right before Doug was settling in to bed, often caught off-guard in nothing but a pair of boxer shorts. Trey eyed him with a vicious hunger that made Doug blush and feel a twisted gnarl in his stomach, and before he opened the window he would pull on a pair of shorts and a t-shirt, despite Trey's objections that he liked looking at the flat pinch of Doug's belly button and the muscled folds beneath his nipples.

One night Doug handed Trey a vial, cylindrical and stoppered. He'd filched it from the chemistry lab.

"What's this?"

The vial was filled with a dark purple liquid, a combination of crushed peonies, periwinkle, a teaspoon of cranberry juice, and a quarter cup of cow's blood; Doug had defrosted a pound of ground beef his mother had swaddled in aluminum foil, hoping too much fat or gristle hadn't wheedled through when he siphoned off the brownish liquid.

"I found a recipe on the internet."

"And?" Trey held the vial up to the light, tilting it so the liquid sloshed back and forth.

"It's supposed to cure vampirism."

Trey lowered his hand and stared at Doug.

"Why would I want to be cured?"

Doug felt a sour tinge in the back of his throat. "Well, you could go back to normal."

"Normal?"

Trey said nothing and passed the vial back to Doug, who, when Trey left, poured it down the bathroom sink.

Every time, Trey would ask the same questions, wondering aloud if Doug was ready yet. Doug kept saying no even though he relished how close Trey sat, perched on the end of his bed, the nutty smell of Trey's breath washing over him when Trey leaned in toward Doug's throat, his hand resting on Doug's hip. Trey always looked perturbed when Doug said no, but he kept coming back, speaking with patience, a rushed kindness that Doug knew was forced.

"Why not?" Trey finally said. "You did it to me first."

"About that," Doug said, but then wasn't sure what to say next. He'd scoured the internet for the various ways one became a vampire, had learned everything he could find about the lore and myths, but there was nothing about a non-vampire turning someone else into a vampire.

"I still have a reflection," Doug said. "I can go outside when it's sunny."

They were sitting in Trey's car. He'd offered to fly through the night with Doug clinging to his back but Doug had declined, citing a desire to actually be able to have a conversation. They'd settled in their spot blocks away from Doug's house, the ranches along both sides of the street dark except for the occasional low lamp visible through drawn Venetian blinds.

"So?" Trey said.

"So how can you be sure I did this to you?"

Trey blinked and bared his fangs, which Doug was pretty sure Trey had sharpened somehow; his canines were slimmer and more scythe-like.

"How else do you explain it?" Trey said, tickling his fingers against his neck. The skin had long healed, no sign of Doug's bite remaining on Trey's throat.

"I guess I can't, really. But I'm still pretty sure you have to be a vampire to make a vampire."

"Well," Trey said, "maybe I'm not a vampire. Maybe I'm something else."

"But you exhibit all the signs of vampirism."

"Looking like something and being something aren't the same thing."

"That's true," Doug said.

Trey asked again if Doug was ready to be transformed, his voice assuming a low growl that Doug had figured out was meant to be alluring more so than frightening, though it was becoming cartoonish the more Trey employed it. He looked Doug in the eye, and Doug felt a tugging deep in his spinal column, an urgent need rushing through his nervous system, a whisper telling him that yes, he did want Trey to bite him. But then Doug snapped out of it.

"I'm just not sure," Doug said, laying a hand on Trey's where it clutched the steering wheel. "I'm not ready for that."

"You don't want to be like me," Trey said, his voice falling, eyes lowered.

"That's not true," Doug said.

"Then what?"

"I don't know."

Trey sighed and started the ignition. He let Doug out a few houses down, as usual, then sped off. Doug waited that night for Trey to tap at the window, clinging and grinning, but he never showed.

‡

It happened when Doug's parents were out of town. Trey came through the front door, courteous enough to knock even though it was unlocked. They sat on the living room sofa, arms around one another, and watched football, a college game between two schools no one cared about; after all, it was a Friday night, and the high-powered division one teams vying for the national title only played on Saturdays.

Doug's hand wandered to Trey's chest. Trey still breathed even though he didn't need to—he liked, he said, to feel the expansion of his ribs and the cascade of oxygen through his nostrils—but his heart did not beat; where in the past Doug had felt the heavy thud-thump when he pressed a hand to Trey's sternum and could feel the pulse of blood through his neck or even his wrist, Trey's body had turned into a cold, unresponsive thing, stoic like a bank vault and more like a slab of thick meat than a living, moving creature.

Trey laid his hand over Doug's and leaned back, taking Doug with him so they were parallel on the couch, Trey's body behind Doug's, ankles tangled together like bougainvillea, Trey's kneecaps pressing against Doug's hamstrings. Trey still smelled like Trey, his voluntary breath filled with his nutty scent; he had spritzed himself with his father's cologne and so Doug's nose was filled with the salty tang of the ocean. Doug felt a warm rapture, an intense wish that this could be his everyday life, that at parties he and Trey could let their fingers wander together like other couples did, that they could saunter down the hall at school like the pairs of movie-star-attractive soccer players and their cheerleader girlfriends, hands cupped around waists and lips pecking at cheeks and mouths.

"Have you thought about it more?" Trey finally said, his voice a low buzzing grumble against Doug's head.

"I just don't know," he said.

Trey's body tensed and he slid out from behind Doug, snaking up so he was suddenly atop him. Their configuration changed before Doug could process it. Trey towered over him, his legs locked around Doug's.

"It'll be fine," Trey said. "I promise."

Trey stared down at Doug, his eyes wide and unblinking, and once again Doug felt that urge to give in, a melting heat spreading through his body that relaxed his muscles and calmed the frantic synapses firing in his brain. It was the opposite of what he used to feel in Trey's presence, when his breath would sharpen, blood pounding through him like he was listening to the whoosh of the ocean. He would pinch himself in the thigh to fend off the throbbing erections that would plague him if he and Trey touched for too long. This, on the other hand, was a cerulean, washing feeling, as if he'd swallowed painkillers and was floating on a dissociative buzz.

Trey leaned in, keeping his eyes on Doug. He cuffed Doug's arm, his grip tight and forceful as he lowered himself, squashing Doug into the couch's plushy cushions. When Trey broke his stare with Doug and lowered his head toward Doug's neck, the yielding wallow in Doug's body snapped away, torn like a stripped bandage, and he felt a sudden nauseated fear, his ears flooding with an oceanic whoosh of blood.

He tried yelling out, but Trey wasn't listening. Doug felt the hot stickiness of Trey's lips against his neck and was, for once, not aroused, but instead disgusted and worried and terrified. When his continued yelps did no good, he instinctively brought his free hand up in a fist and smashed it against Trey's temple.

Trey crumpled. He tumbled off the couch, wedged against the coffee table whose glass top cracked when Trey's elbow clipped it as he fell. Trey was trapped long enough for Doug to pole vault his way over Trey and into the kitchen. He padded through the junk drawer where his mother, thankfully, had once stuck a plastic beaded rosary, which Doug yanked out and held before him.

When Trey stood he stared at Doug then shook his head, holding his hands up in surrender.

"I told you I wasn't ready," Doug said, his voice a hoarse hiss. He lowered the rosary but clutched it, letting the sharp edges of the cut plastic beads slice into his skin like little teeth nipping at the soft flesh of his palms. He was washed in sadness as if a pet had died.

Before Doug could ask him to leave, Trey was gone, zipping out of the house like a flash, leaving the door sagging open like a lolling jaw.

‡

Trey showed up at school one last time a week later. He was covered in thick layers of fabric, sunglasses with lenses the size of coffee cups covering his eyes, a scarf layered like a queen's collar around his neck, a knit cap pulled tight over his head as if it had been vacuum sealed against his skull.

His arm was slung over one of the cheerleaders, a leggy brunette known for wearing skirts even in the coldest weather; today she was sieved up in tight jeans, her face covered in the same accessories drooped over Trey.

Doug felt a tight coil as Trey and the cheerleader passed him. Time seemed to slow, and Trey, raising a hand clad in a leather biker's glove, pulled down the massive sunglasses just enough to make eye contact with Doug. Doug thought he saw a shiny sadness there, but then the girl did the same, smirking. Together, Trey and the girl flashed him toothy grins, revealing identical pairs of fangs.

Doug said nothing. He watched them march straight down the hall past the math classrooms, pull a sharp right, and slink in the direction of the front lobby, and the front door, and the parking lot, and their freedom. He pictured Trey and the girl flying through the night, hands locked, bodies tingling with weightlessness. Doug felt a pang of sadness knowing he would never feel Trey's lips on his again, never know the touch of their hands on one another's shoulders or quadriceps. The earthy smell of Trey's breath would never press his earlobes.

Now, though, Doug would wait, and nibble away at someone only when he was ready to be nipped back.

BOYS WITH FACES LIKE MIRRORS

The bus crash devastated everyone.

That morning, Jane Philban looked out the kitchen window and tsked at the thunder heads perched above the trees. Her son bounced on the balls of his feet behind her, telling her it didn't matter because the field trip was to the bowling alley, and the bowling alley had a roof.

Mrs. Pederson's son pleaded from his bed to be allowed to go even though he had a 101-degree fever. He didn't feel sick, he said, slapping at his high forehead and kicking his feet like he was pedaling a bike. I feel fine, and you know I really like the smell of bowling shoes.

Anthony Skiles dressed himself, picking out a t-shirt and the new jeans he'd gotten for his birthday because the field trip meant no one had to put on the blazers or the purple-and-green striped ties they wore every day. His dress shirt was wrinkly, for which the teachers always frowned at him. Anthony waited for the bus while his mother cried in her bedroom because her husband had told her the night before that he wanted a divorce. No one had told Anthony this, but he'd heard a lot of yelling, the slamming of a door, and his mother's sobs. He'd reheated his own dinner.

The story was all over the news that night: the bus skidding across a wet slick on the highway overpass and careening through the cement guardrail down into traffic below. No one on board survived, except the driver, who was in a coma for three weeks. She made a full recovery except for some nerve damage in her left leg. Her doctor told her to get a cane, but she refused, and spent the rest of her life dragging one side of her body behind her, pulling the reminder of what had happened with her everywhere she went like a sand bag.

The first funeral—Catholic, with a closed casket—was a week after the crash. All of the school administrators came, wearing somber black suits. The principal wore a swishing, heavy dress that drooped over the pew. She sat near the back and had to excuse herself when she started to hyperventilate. The night before she'd written in her journal that she was terrified of funerals, that they made her feel like an empty vase.

It was during the funeral mass that the pounding noise started. Through their tears, the parents of the dead boy looked around, startled. The father wasn't crying but the mother was, her mascara running tracks down her cheeks. When it became clear that the pounding was coming from the casket, she screamed and fainted like something from an old movie. Her husband caught her and trembled, staring toward the box holding their son. The priest stopped and whispered to one of the altar servers, who shook her head.

The priest opened the casket, which creaked like a falling tree. Everyone started screaming when the boy sat up, even men who would swear on their lives that they'd never once ever made such a noise.

The dead boys were alive again. After the initial shock, and when, three funerals later, people realized that this was happening to all of the boys, mothers waiting for their children's re-awakenings pulled their sons to their chests when they sat up in their caskets. Fathers pinched the bridges of their noses and tried to breathe deeply. Siblings cried or swayed, hands in pockets, unsure of what to do. Those who were older stared at their shoes and grabbed at their shirt collars or the hems of their skirts.

Not all of the boys came back, and neither did the three parental chaperones or the math teacher who had been aboard the bus. Armin Stabler and his twin brother Adam were the last boys scheduled for burial, a dual funeral, and their mother hiccoughed and fanned herself when one son—Adam—stretched out his arms like he was just waking for school. She and her husband waited for Armin to stir as well, but he never did. His lips remained pursed, eyes closed. Because everyone expected them to both be reborn, hardly anyone came to the service. The church was small, anyway, and the air conditioning was out. The twins' father's shirt stuck to his back. There weren't enough men to carry Armin's coffin out, so his brother joined the pallbearers, trying to heft his brother's weight in his newly-resurrected arms. The casket swayed and dipped toward the ground.

The boys seemed themselves, had all of their memories. Anthony Skiles remembered that his father had walked out and was surprised to find him at the funeral. He insisted his father come home and smooth things out with Anthony's mother. We should try to make it work, he said, squeezing his wife's bony shoulder. She nodded through tears.

As far as anyone could tell, it was as if nothing had happened to the boys. They were human beings, certainly, nothing like the mindless zombies on television or in the movies. Doctors poked and prodded at them. They listened to the boys' heartbeats with their stethoscopes, and the boys winced at the cold metal on their skin. None of them had any scars; their injuries were healed. The few that had been young organ donors were whole again, their hearts and lungs regrown in their chest cavities. They all said they felt fine. Their temperatures were normal.

But something was wrong with their eyes.

Yes, they all said when asked if they could see, confusion in their voices. They had no problems following their physicians' pen lights, and they squinted and squirmed when the brightness was drawn in close. But their eyes looked wrong.

They're like mirrors, one mother said, finally, bending in close to her son, who wiggled uncomfortably on the doctor's pleather seat, the sanitary paper crinkling under him. Her nose reflected back in her boy's eyes, which were a shimmering silver color. She waved her hands back and forth and the glimmer of her skin flashed across his face.

Are they cataracts? she offered.

No, the doctor said. Not milky enough.

She leaned in close to her son's right eye. Hmm, she said.

Please don't do that, her son said. Can we go home yet? I'm getting cold.

When asked to look at themselves in the bathroom mirror, none of the boys saw anything out of the ordinary. Mrs. Pederson bit her lip and glanced at her husband, who shrugged. What? their son said. What's wrong? He blinked and his eyes caught the overhead light, twinkling.

None of the boys had any memory of the crash itself. Just the skidding and screaming and the large thumping noise of the bus smashing through the cement barrier, which had crumbled like a soft cookie. Then waking up in itchy black suits and stuffed into boxes. They talked about their experience in interviews for the major news networks. Diane Sawyer, Al Roker, Katie Couric even, spoke with the boys and their families, their talks sprinkled over the following weeks, the boys with their mirror eyes sitting at an angle to the camera. In voiceover, with images wafting across the screen—the bus crunched up like an accordion, EMTs running around with windblown hair—Brian Williams or George Stephanopoulos said that doctors had no explanation for the boys' eyes, much less why they were alive.

Life returned to something like normal. Parents tucked their boys into bed with extra care. They drove with the radio turned off and their hands tight against the steering wheel. When it rained, parents bit their lips and some kept their boys home from school. Jane Philban shook her head and told her husband, as he stepped out of the shower, that she'd told him so. She could say that now, now that their son was alive and not dead: she'd told him so. She'd stared out the window and known those rain clouds were trouble.

Mr. Philban and the other husbands had sex with their wives in celebration and relief. This seemed to them the most normal course of action, because what else was there to do? Their bodies and brains were flummoxed from being overwhelmed by inconsolability and then elation. They found themselves waking up in the middle of the night unsure if their sons' resurrections had been a dream, and they often tip-toed down the hallway, scuffling across the shag carpet, to press open bedroom doors and peer in, assuring themselves that the lumpiness under the covers was an actual living boy and not a trick of the shadows and moonlight.

I hold my breath every morning when I wake him up, one mother said to another. I'm worried he's going to disappear again.

I honestly can't look at them, their English teacher said while having a drink at a bar that smelled like grease and cheese and whose dim light hid the sticky stains on the tile floor. She was talking to some guy she barely knew. She took a drag on a cigarette. They all pay perfectly good attention, which is unnerving in ten-year-old boys. And I don't think they blink anymore. Just stare, stare, stare.

For an entire year, nothing happened to the boys. Not one of them was seriously hurt or sick, as if they were invincible. Their parents accepted their sons' eyes, a spot of compromise, many of them thought. An acceptable mutation for the sake of their being alive. Sure, they were all quieter, more subdued. Most of the ones who had played soccer or basketball shrugged when sign-ups rolled around, saying they would rather read, or sit on the couch, or sleep. Those who had loved video games found themselves staring up from their beds, where they retreated after dinner, counting the gritty lumps in the popcorn ceilings. When one parent worried aloud, saying something was different, wrong almost, another would clamp down on the worrier's hand with a squeeze, saying it was true. Things aren't the same, but how could they be? At least we have them. At least there's that.

Right, the other would say, voice drifting like condensation.

School was cancelled on the anniversary of the accident, but there was a memorial for the math teacher and the other adults, along with Armin Stabler, whose mother had been all but forgotten. Her husband had left, unable to deal with the withering gloom that descended over the house. Adam Stabler spent most of his time in the lower bunk bed in his room, the place where his brother had slept. He rolled toward the wall, greeting his mother with a curved-in shoulder when she tried to say good night to him. They ate meals in silence, his mirrored eyes glued to his undercooked mashed potatoes.

The memorial was held on the school soccer field. Everyone sat in long rows of white wooden folding chairs that gave people splinters if they weren't careful. The boys sat with their parents, rather than in the front as originally planned, at the quiet request of the mayor, who was the guest speaker. He'd been struck by an eerie shudder any time he imagined twenty-four boys with faces like mirrors staring up at him in the sunshine, their noses and mouths obscured by the shining light blistering from their faces. He spoke of gratitude and loss and consolation and not taking things for granted. Everyone sitting near the husband of the dead math teacher reached out and squeezed various body parts, and eventually he started squirming and cried out for everyone to stop touching him and he stood and marched off the field while everyone stared. People turned back around a few minutes later and waited for the mayor to finish speaking. They processed one by one to the front and laid roses on a table in front of blown-up photographs of the dead.

That night, parents were shocked when they tucked their boys into bed. A round robin of phone calls revealed that yes, Jane Philban's son, and Anita Pederson's son, and Betty Skiles'

Anthony all had a strange silver sheen to their skin, like someone had covered their faces in metallic paint.

He looks like the Tin Man, Mrs. Philban whispered to herself. She tried wiping at her son's cheek, but he grunted and slapped her hand away and turned toward the wall.

What do we do, she said.

Take him to the doctor, I guess, her husband said.

A few parents took their sons to the emergency room that night, only to have harried doctors tell them that this was something new, something never-before-seen, and that there wasn't a prescribed treatment for this. Temperatures were normal, double and triple checked. Blood pressures stable, heartbeats strong, steady thumps in chests. The boys reported a slight itchiness in their faces, and, in an attempt to assuage unnerved parents, the doctors suggested Benadryl and a good night's sleep.

In the morning, parents were greeted with sons whose faces had changed. Although the shape was the same, their cheekbones, lips, everything had taken on the hue of a mirror, glassy and sleek. The contours of the boys' faces made their parents' reflections stretch and bloat like they were staring into a funhouse mirror. Terrified, the parents called one another.

I don't know what to do.

No one will tell me what's going on.

Me neither.

Are you sending him to school?

How can I?

One mother lamented to her therapist: I just want to see him, but all I can see is myself.

It was the start of some unstoppable devolution. The next day, the mirror coldness had strayed down to the boys' chests and into their hair; a week later, they were walking mirrors, shimmering back everything around them. Parents could barely look at them, the images were so confusing. The boys continued to say they felt nothing amiss in their bones. Their hands still felt like hands. When they rolled their tongues over their lips, they felt the smooth roundness of flesh, the familiar ridges of their mouths. They could move and walk and talk as always. In their own eyes, they looked absolutely normal. All of them did complain of an even stronger urge to sleep, an exhaustion that was starting to heave down on their shoulders like heavy hands. Most of them stopped going to school and only sat up in bed for some soup or cereal.

It's getting unbearable, Jane Philban lamented to her husband one night while they were wrapped in each other's arms.

I just wish there was something we could do, said Mrs. Pederson.

Anthony Skiles' mother and father started fighting again, the stress of what was happening to their son opening up cracks they had tried to cleave together upon his return from the dead. They managed to whisper at first, keeping their hissing disagreement from their son's reflective ears, but volume started to edge its way into their voices without them noticing.

When their skin from head to foot had taken on the sheen of a mirror, the boys were sleeping almost all day. One couldn't tell if their eyes were open or closed anymore; even their eyelashes were tiny, flicking mirrors. The Philbans stood watch over their son, taking vacation and sick days in order to be near him. His breathing was heavy and creaky, and it fogged his mirror-lips with each exhalation. They watched him toss and turn, groaning that there was a heavy weight on his chest.

Doctors still couldn't account for what was happening. Aside from the scraping clink of metal on metal, stethoscopes revealed nothing but a normal heartbeat, if a little slower than before. Blood pressure was still normal—and, to many doctors' surprise, still detectable through cold metallic arms—and temperatures stable. X-rays revealed regular skeletons underneath that glassy, reflective exterior.

After a week of this shining transformation, parents woke to an unsettled calm. The nervousness that had become a sourness in their mouths and a stiffness in their arms was gone. The Philbans and Pedersons rushed to their sons' rooms; Mr. and Mrs. Skiles—he from the living room, her from their California king bed—met in the hallway and felt their looming distaste for one another vanish like rising mist. Husbands and wives went together to their sons, letting bedroom doors creak open like vault entrances, heavy and safe. Though their sons' beds were tousled, blankets and sheets twisted with the unsettled sleep they knew had befallen their children, something was smooth and kind about the comforters' slopes.

They peeled back the blankets and found mirrors lying there. Nothing boy-shaped, but flat, body-length mirrors with plain wooden borders stained the color of their sons' hair. The parents looked these mirrors up and down, peeling the covers all the way back.

None of them cried out or bawled. Mrs. Stabler let a few tears dribble down her face, and they plunked against the cold metal that had once been her son. No one suspected some kind of trick. Jane Philban squeezed her husband's hand and let out a small sigh, a release of air that had been bottled up for the past year.

Together, parents lifted the mirrors from the beds. The wood was smooth in their hands, warm. They squeezed the frames hard, feeling their own pulses in their clenched fists. Each couple chose a spot: above the fireplace, in the dining room, on the bedroom wall: somewhere to hang their mirror, a place they would pass by regularly, somewhere to stop, chew on a cheek, and, looking themselves over, adjusting a collar or tie, smoothing a shirt, remember.

HAPPY BIRTHDAYS

When he told the woman behind the counter he wanted two slices of the German chocolate, she said, "Are you sure?" and he said, "Yes," and she said, "Okay. I just have to make sure," and he said, "I'm sure," and she said, "My boss just wants to make sure everyone is sure," and he nodded, and she said, "Because he only wants happy customers," and he said, "I'm sure," and she gave him a long, scrutinizing look and then said, "Okay," and cut him two slices of the German chocolate and set them in two of the bakery's sapphire-blue boxes and handed them to him across the counter and said, "And that's it?" and he said, "Yep," so she told him how much and he paid her and she said, "See you again soon," and it wasn't a question because she knew, and he knew, that he would, in fact, be back.

He took the pieces home and set them on dinner plates, too large for single slices, and added forks at weird angles to occupy some of the white space, and then he waited, and when his husband came home they sat down in the dining room and they ate, and they didn't speak as they ate, and even though they rarely ate sugary things, they each ate every bit, even the crumbs that fell from their lips, and even though neither of them liked coconut the cake was good, but neither said so, because that wasn't the point, and then, when they were finished, they sat and waited and they didn't say a word about why they were eating the cake, or waiting, because they both knew why, and even though the reason was terrible and superficial they had agreed it was important to both of them to know, and so they let themselves change, and they stared at each other's faces as they grew older, wrinkles etching into the corners of their eyes, shoulders slouching and losing muscle mass, hair thinning and going gray, throats loosening, stomachs going slack, elbows turning chalky and dry.

"Do you think that's it?" he said, and his husband said, "Probably close enough," and he said, "So this is—" and his husband said, "I guess so," and they stood, both of them feeling it in their joints, and they turned around several times for examination, and then his husband started unbuttoning his shirt, and he said, "In the dining room?" and his husband said, "It really did work, didn't it?" and they left the dining room and climbed the stairs to the second floor, taking the steps one at a time, leaning against the banister, the skin of their knuckles cracking, knees hot and tight like petrified wood, and in their bedroom they peeled their clothes off on opposite sides of their California king, and they were upset by the wiry hairs on their sternums, they were upset by the slouchy wrinkles around their belly buttons, they were upset by the disappearance of their abs, they were upset by the shapelessness of their hips, they were upset by the droopiness of their balls, and they didn't bother with sex or kissing, fearing the papery feel of one another's lips, the slip-slide of their backs, and they groaned in tandem as they pulled up their pants and they wrenched their shoulders putting on their shirts, and they went back downstairs, complaining of the effort and pain in their bones at the descent, and they drove right back to the bakery.

The woman grinned and said, "Hello, again," and then she said, "What can I get you?" and she set her forearms on the top of the glass case, and they frowned toward the sponges and chiffons and biscuit cake, at the simple chocolate and the genoise and buttermilk and sad lemon, and seeing that they were taking a long time squinting and looking she said, "The simple white will do the job," and she said, "Shall I cut you two slices?" and they nodded and she said, "Should I bother boxing them?" and he shook his head even though his husband seemed to think about it for a moment, too long, he thought, and then he paid and she handed them over and he grabbed his slice up without using the fork she provided and he ate, and he ignored the sugar and the fat and the buttery flavor and swallowed the slice practically whole, and he glanced at his husband who was careful and took his time, who actually used his fork, who seemed to savor each bite, but he didn't say a word, and instead he handed the woman his empty plate, and she threw it away, and he tried to see himself in the glass but all he could see was the black forest cake and the cheesecake and the pineapple upside down cake, each one with a number next to it, a guidepost, a point in time, some of them far away in the future and some in the ignominious past, and so he stood up straight and waited, and the woman said, "It might take a while," and she said, "Going back is always slower," and his husband took his hand and led him out to the car, and his husband drove, carefully, slowly, and they didn't speak, and despite what she'd said by the time they were home he felt like himself again, and he said so, and his husband said, "Isn't every version of us a version of ourselves?" and he didn't say anything in response but he didn't think so, he wasn't sure, to be honest, he wasn't convinced that anything was set in stone, but he didn't want to say that because his husband was a philosopher, a good one, a smart one, and he knew he would lose any argument that was epistemological or metaphysical or ontological or not based on numbers, which were what he knew, round and straight and hard and always simple in their singular answers.

He followed his husband inside.

They took the stairs without a word and went to their sides of the bed and took off their clothes and kissed and touched and felt the tightness of their muscles that they had both worked so hard for and they raked their fingers through one another's thick hair and moaned and had sex and orgasmed and laid together staring at the ceiling breathing wet hard breaths and they laced their fingers together into an indistinguishable knot and they kissed and played footsie and laughed and pretended they had not seen what they had seen as if they didn't know what was coming and they fell asleep and the next day they woke up and didn't talk about it and didn't suggest going back to the bakery and eating more cake because that was too much and too hard and it was so much easier to be who they were now and to not try to remember or predict because the past was the past and the future was the future and the now was now and the now was good, it was where they were and where they wanted to be, and agreeing about that took no words, no gestures, no nothing, no talk, no touch, no trouble, it was, as they say, a piece of cake.

WHERE CAN I TAKE YOU WHEN THERE'S NOWHERE TO GO

Even though Peter Vanderwaal told us not to bring gifts to his birthday party, we all knew Roddy DeCosta would show up with a box, wrapped in shiny paper, containing one of his clouds.

The party was actually a week after Peter's eighteenth birthday because his parents were out of town and his stoner cousin Gage could buy a keg and enough Popov for hundreds of Jell-O shots that he and Peter chilled in the refrigerator, moving the milk and cold cuts out onto the front porch where the frigid February Missouri air kept them cool. Peter lived off one of the state highways that wound through the rural capillaries northwest of St. Louis, a thirty-plus minute drive for most of us, who lived in Clayton and the Central West End. But we liked Peter's house, situated on acres of farmland his parents rented out to the neighbors because they had no idea how to manage rows of corn and soybeans. The yard was good for bonfires with a generous fire pit and held a huge net-encased trampoline, an elaborate treehouse that was a good place to hook up, and a small yurt, made of canvas and cross-hatched beech, which his younger brother had erected as part of his Eagle Scout project.

Everyone loved Peter, who was the swim team captain. He had the right kind of body for it, lean in the waist but thick in the shoulders. That's why he went to school with us, so far away from his house when there were plenty of other St. Louis academies and public high schools in between: our coach had a reputation for sending student athletes to the best programs in the country, and had even produced a few Olympians whose photos hung in the natatorium. Peter had been recruited by Texas and Florida and Cal as early as our freshman year; he'd missed a bunch of school for campus visits in the last two years and had decided to go to Georgia. He always smelled of chlorine, but on him it was like cologne instead of chemical. His hair was flowy and beachy and blond-streaked.

Most of us arrived at eight or nine even though Peter had told us Gage would arrive with the beer by seven; we had to satiate our parents with family dinner. They didn't really care what we did, so long as we promised not to drink and drive and that if we did anything besides slosh Smirnoff or Bud Select down our throats that we would use protection or make sure the quantities we smoked or snorted weren't deadly. We were the children of lawyers and accountants, hedge fund managers who didn't know what to do with us except set us up with trust funds and easy access to private colleges and universities via large donations for new fine arts buildings or at least renovated dormitory wings.

Roddy DeCosta showed up at 9:15 with his black hair slicked back, a bomber jacket tight around his shoulders, his Vans dirty as usual, the right one's sole flapping and falling apart. No one could tell if he was trying to appear cool by arriving so late or not; Roddy had a reputation for charging into school after the bell for homeroom had rung, and he was constantly serving detentions for "egregious tardiness," as our demerit reports, which went home with us every three months and we all forged our parents' signatures on, said. But we knew Roddy's parents didn't care. They both worked as phlebotomy techs at Barnes-Jewish and were hardly ever home, leaving Roddy alone in their tiny apartment on Arsenal, where we knew he and his mom and dad lived in a cramped two-bedroom above a Bosnian family that was constantly using the communal grill behind the building to roast cevapi and pljeskavica. Roddy played basketball and was the starting point guard for our team, which wasn't very good. But Roddy stood out, handling the ball with aplomb, staying low, threading it between his legs, crossing up opposing defenses with his fast feet and surprisingly good outside shot. He was a scholarship kid; even his uniforms had been donated or paid for by some kind of endowment. He rarely spoke in class, but when he did, people listened. Everyone knew he was smart because of the way he talked about feminist criticism and demonstrated a mastery of Derrida in AP English. He mostly kept to himself, writing stories during study hall in a Moleskine. Rumor was that he'd had a few of them published in literary magazines, and not just our shitty student-run one that Mr. Harker, the faculty adviser, was always trying to get Roddy to contribute to or even run as editor-in-chief. Roddy always said no, for whatever reason. He was a mystery none of us had ever cracked.

‡

When Roddy arrived, Peter was already feeling tingly and light thanks to the bowl Gage had made him smoke. He didn't usually go in for that, using his swim training as an excuse, laughing and mumbling about his lung capacity and endurance. Because of his reputation and the whispers about his upward trajectory, people let it go; as long as he was his smiling, gregarious self, people let Peter do whatever he wanted. When Gage offered to underwrite the party, Peter couldn't say no. Gage promised not to invite any of his drinking buddies, who were also his drug-using buddies, who were also the kind of people who wouldn't respect Peter's embargo on going inside beyond the mudroom off the side of the house. They were the kind of people who would bring more serious stuff than weed to a stranger's house. Gage was good at keeping his promises, though, so when he said, "Invite list is all you, bro," Peter believed him.

Peter watched his classmates come stomping up the angled driveway and around the side of the house, girls in skirts way too short or sheer—or both—for the weather, guys bundled up in cardigans and Henleys, some of them with the sleeves rolled to their elbows. All of his classmates looked the same, he thought. They all wanted the same things—booze and drugs, and eventually four years at expensive universities that their parents cared about more than they did—and he was, frankly, bored by the thought of a night with them around. Though he would never admit it, he really only cared about seeing Roddy.

‡

Roddy first made a name for himself in third grade when, during a unit on clouds, he started creating them. Elbows propped on his desk, hands curled in a bowl like he was cupping them to catch water, he was listening to Ms. Miller's voice, soft and puffy just like the clouds she was describing. Roddy pictured one of them there in his palms, gathered out of the air to swirl above his fingers, and then suddenly, there it was: a little cumulus the size of a softball. He heard giggling behind him, but didn't turn to look. He let the cloud dissipate, which took no more effort than imagining it crumbling into the air. Then he pictured a cirrus, thready and thin and ethereal, and there it was, too. The laughter grew louder, crescendoing when he made a little cumulonimbus that croaked out a tiny peal of lightning that sounded like a finger-snap and was followed by a little boom of thunder like the noise of a door slammed two rooms away. Ms. Miller looked around and saw Roddy, sitting in his seat in the row nearest the window, two desks back, and asked what he was doing. When he blinked and said, "Making clouds," she looked ready to faint. His parents were called, not understanding what was wrong, and then he was gone for weeks, hauled around to specialists, doctors, even scientists, who all shrugged and confirmed what Roddy had said: he made clouds.

As he got older, the clouds got larger. Classmates made requests. They asked him to summon up storms that would short the electricity on campus so they could get out of class early. They begged for snow the night before big history tests or rain in advance of the compulsory mile runs for Presidential fitness. But Roddy shook his head every time, saying he couldn't do anything that big. He didn't really know, but he was afraid to try. After that first cloud, which had felt so light and glorious between his hands, his parents sat down with him and told him: *Be careful.* He was sitting on the edge of his bed, heels knocking against the frame. His father squatted in front of him, looking tired. His mother, in the chair that sat shoved against his tiny writing desk, looked afraid. He knew how hard they worked, and as they told him he needed to keep the clouds to himself, he stared down at his hands. He frowned, wondering how something that had made him feel so nice—pinpricked with light, breezy with the gauzy wisps that emerged from his fingertips—could be something he had to hide.

‡

We stood around with our plastic cups in our hands, our vision swimming, bodies warmed against the night by the alcohol. We watched Roddy scan the dark for Peter, who was finishing a keg stand, his sweater riding up to show off his lean swimmer's torso. Gage was chanting out Peter's time, reaching twenty-one, twenty-two, twenty-three, twenty-four, twenty-five. Peter kicked his legs and his teammates Bo Durgle and Mike Partridge lowered him to the ground. Peter wiped his mouth with the sleeve of his shirt, let out a loud belch, received hooted applause, and blinked into the dark.

Gage was wearing a sleeveless t-shirt despite the cold, his left arm covered in tattoos, vague swirls of green and blue and yellow topped, along his deltoid, with Chinese characters that he probably thought meant something like "Peace and Knowledge" but probably really translated to something like "Dog fart soup." Gage had gone to high school with our older brothers and sisters and despite his shitty grades in the most rudimentary English and history and bio classes he'd scored a 35 on the ACT; his PSATs were good enough for a National Merit Scholarship, if only he'd had any interest in college. Besides selling pot and shrooms to teenagers, he was on the payroll at his father's company, which did something with supply chain management, but we were pretty sure Gage wasn't asked to do anything even close to a nine-to-five job, nothing that involved a desk or a tie. Both of his ears were punched with studs that glinted when they caught the floodlight perched over the back of the garage. He winked at Roddy, who looked down at his hands, still holding the box.

Peter took the gift and Roddy took the beer Gage held out for him.

"Heavier than I'd have thought," Peter said. Roddy only nodded in response. Then, while Peter peeled back the paper, careful not to tear it, fishing an index finger beneath a loose flap and slowly pulling the adhesive away, Roddy drank. Those of us nearby saw the slight tremor in his hands, the nervy way the surface of the piss-yellow liquid shivered. He took a long, hard gulp, his face pinching in at the shitty, metallic taste. We didn't see Roddy at many parties. We didn't know what kind of drinker he was. But he finished that first beer before Peter had shimmied the paper off the box and when he held out the cup for a refill, Gage, grinning like a satyr, happily provided.

‡

The box, beneath its wrapping, was plain cardboard. Peter folded the glossy green paper into a neat square and tucked it into his jeans pocket. He licked his lips, tasting the tart beer and the burning shots that his fellow swim team members had plied him with. They'd practically drained a flask down his throat immediately upon their arrival.

He had watched Roddy handling his clouds for years, kids cornering him after school or in the cafeteria, not demanding, exactly, that he make them, but begging, an edge of command in their voices. Roddy always acquiesced, spinning them out of nothing like he was making cotton candy but without the vat of superheated sugar and hot air. Sometimes he would pass them on to whoever had made the request, moving clouds into their cupped hands with the care one might hold a Fabergé egg or a Ninfea sculpture. Peter never asked for one, though he felt a hard yearning to feel Roddy's hands, to know what their folds and lines and fingertips felt like. What magic, he thought, must live there.

The box's edges were held down by mail tape. Peter looked at Roddy and said, "Help?"

Roddy passed his cup to Gage. He slid his hands under the box. Peter, feeling everyone's eyes on him, swallowed and tried to hide the nerve tingling through his limbs. He kept one hand on the top of the box as he pulled at the tape, pressing down so nothing escaped. Then, finally, with an approving nod from Roddy, he pried the upper flaps apart, slow and careful, as if a precious kitten might leap from the inside.

Nothing came flying out, nor did any cirrus or stratus dissipate into the air. Peter looked down into the box and frowned.

"Go on," Roddy said.

Peter dipped his hands in and pulled out what looked like a crystal ball, a little bigger than a softball. Inside was a thick puff of white, like cotton.

"Cumulus," Roddy said. "I remember you saying it was your favorite."

Peter turned the glass ball in both hands. He and Roddy had spent little time together, though Peter had caught sight of Roddy at swim meets, sitting by himself at the top of the wooden bleachers that the small cadre of enthusiastic fans liked to stomp on. Peter, as he knifed through the water during the freestyle, could hear the thrumming like he was in the center of an earthquake. His eyes would always flick toward Roddy when he breached the surface after the final touch, ignoring the clapping of his coaches and cheers of his teammates and fans, able to look to where Roddy sat without detection, eyes occluded by the dark tint of his goggles. Roddy was never clapping, but he was always looking right down at Peter, eyes warm and congratulatory even if his hands were like stones.

He held the globe up to his face.

"I do love cumulus."

Roddy shrugged. "You mentioned it in grade school."

"You remembered after all this time."

"Yeah," Roddy said. "All this time."

‡

When Peter asked if Roddy would come with him to put the cloud away inside—"For safety's sake"—Roddy didn't hesitate to nod *yes*, but inside his jacket and behind his ribs his heart was thudding like he'd swallowed a gallon of Red Bull. In the mud room, Roddy kicked off his shoes without being asked, and he caught how this made Peter smile.

"I like your house," he said.

"Have you ever been inside before?"

"No."

Peter laughed, but it was kind. He waved for Roddy to follow him through the mud room. The farmhouse was all dark oak and wide archways, a baby grand piano tucked into the corner of the great room whose leather sofa was buttressed by marble-topped tables upon which sat Ellard lamps. The wooly staircase was freshly vacuumed, a smell Roddy loved. He gripped the banister tight, his legs wobbly with alcohol. He'd watched Peter guzzle beer, upside down, and was in awe of the way he took the stairs two at a time, leaping with the grace of a gazelle. When Peter turned to watch Roddy take the last half of the staircase one step at a time, Roddy felt like he was lit up by a spotlight.

Peter flicked on his bedroom light, contours erupting with shape and color: a clean queen-size bed with rich chocolate quilted comforter and stark white bed skirt, the combination making it look like he slept on a gargantuan ice cream sandwich; a desk built into the wall beneath three spacious shelves that held his many swimming trophies and medals and ribbons; framed photos arrayed at different heights around the room of Peter in his swimming gear, arms dotted with liquid, his Speedo revealing the cut of his hipbones and the long roll of muscle that scrolled from belly button to ribs; a neat dresser where a photograph of his family sat above a drawer left slightly ajar, the elastic edges of boxer shorts sticking out.

Roddy tried not to look at the photos, or the underwear. If Peter felt strange having Roddy in this intimate space, he didn't show it. Peter was staring at his bureau, one finger pressed to his lips, which were slitted open the width of a coin, his other hand hugging the cloud and its globe to his right hip.

"This is the right spot," Peter said. He turned. "Don't you think?"

"I think it should be wherever you want it."

"That's sweet."

Roddy felt his cheeks redden. He sat on the end of the bed. "Your photos are cool."

"My parents did that." Peter shook his head. "They pay a photographer to go to my meets. It's embarrassing."

"It shows they care, doesn't it?"

Peter shrugged as he lifted the globe. Roddy remembered putting the cloud in there, how he wasn't sure if it would work, settling the globe—bought at a craft store for more money than he thought a simple glass ball could cost—in his palms, pushing the cloud to the forefront of his mind. Every time was a little different. Sometimes he felt thirsty after, others like he needed to pee. His head throbbed, or he felt buzzed, or like he had just woken from a long, satisfying sleep. His hands trembled after, tips tingling with ice, other times fire, as if he'd been stung by something. He'd felt a long thrill when the cumulus appeared inside the glass; he'd been sure it wouldn't work, but there the cottony purl was, bobbing in the globe.

"They care about what it says about them."

"Sorry?" Roddy looked up from his hands. He felt his cheeks flush.

Peter turned to him and gestured toward the photos. "They're proud of themselves for what they did to make me."

"Make you?"

"I hated swimming as a kid." Peter came and sat down next to Roddy. "But I was so good at it, even from a young age. They made me keep going, convinced me I had a gift." He looked down at his hands, palms up on his thighs. Roddy followed his gaze. "It was their discipline, not mine, that made me what I am."

"Oh."

Peter jolted then, as though he'd been zapped with electricity. "Sorry. Didn't mean to get heavy."

"It's okay."

"It's a party," he said. "I shouldn't ruin the party."

"You're not ruining anything."

"I didn't even want to throw this stupid thing. I hate parties."

"You do?"

Peter stood, nodding. "But what can I do? I can't hide out."

"We could go for a walk," Roddy blurted, then immediately regretted it. But then Peter smiled, a real rosiness in his cheeks.

"Yes," he said. "I'd like that."

‡

As with any party, its purpose evaporated, and instead of worrying about Peter and whether he was enjoying his celebration, we were concerned about keeping our buzzes strong. A cadre of boys started canoe races while the girls filed into the bathroom connected to the mudroom, traveling in small herds to talk and take turns on the toilet. Someone produced a flask, a handful of pills. We didn't ask what they were before popping them onto our tongues and washing them down with hard, lighter flu-id-tasting tequila. Our vision spangled, and someone threw up in the grass. Gage watched, shaking his head and laughing at us. A few of us wandered inside. The kitchen was sparkling clean and smelled of lemon verbena. When we called out, no one answered. Peter's bedroom was dark and empty. Someone flicked on the overhead light.

We weren't sure who picked up the cloud first, but it got passed all around. It landed in each of our hands with a surprising lightness, barely heavier than a beach ball. The glass was cool, the cloud a thick puff of moisture that had left some bits of condensation along the curve. We held it up to our eyes like a telescope, looked at one another through the thick fiber.

"How do you think he does it?" someone said.

"He doesn't know. No one does."

"How do you know that?"

"You think no one's ever asked him?"

"There has to be some explanation."

"Okay, Einstein. What do you think?"

"I don't have a fucking clue."

"Neither do his doctors. I heard he sees doctors all the time."

"Do you think it hurts him to do it?"

"Why would it hurt?"

"Why wouldn't it?"

"I bet he gets to see doctors cheap because of his parents?"

"What about his parents?"

"Working at the hospital."

"Please. They're techs. They're like the busboys of the hospital."

"What, and the servers are so important?"

"Doctors are like the managers, dumbass."

"You think a doctor is like a McDonald's manager?"

"You guys are idiots."

Someone tossed the globe up in the air. The cloud flashed in the light.

"Careful with that thing!"

"It's fine."

"It's not ours. You could break it."

"Chill out."

"Put it back."

"Jesus. Stop hitting me. I'm putting it back."

We set the cloud down on the dresser, arguing about where exactly it had sat. Peter noticed these kinds of things. Some of us had tried to surprise him on his sixteenth birthday, decoding his locker combination and stuffing it full of balloons. Instead of opening it to a spill of inflated rubber, Peter paused before spinning the lock and frowned, saying that he always left it on the number one. We scoffed, but he knew we'd done something. When one of the history teachers showed up without her wedding ring on, Peter stayed after class to ask her if she was okay. He didn't use the word *divorce*, but word spread quickly. Rumor was that she'd broken down crying in front of Peter, and he'd held out a packet of Kleenex that he kept in his backpack, a gesture that only made her sob more.

Eventually we agreed on the placement of the cloud. We stared at it for one more moment before backing out of the room. We slid outside and asked Gage if he would help us with keg stands. We took turns dangling in the air, beer rushing into our mouths, fighting against gravity as we swallowed. The cold was different with our bodies alight, legs kicked upward, dresses threatening to reveal our panties, t-shirts revealing our slabs of belly. We counted out seconds for one another, our voices crashing across the fields. After each turn we clapped and cheered, even for those of us who could only manage a few seconds. We wiped our mouths with the backs of our hands and laughed at our fresh buzzes, at the way the world tilted and teetered as we regained our bearing.

‡

Peter liked walking his rural street at night even though his parents thought it dangerous, as if he wouldn't see headlights coming and would be run over by some wayward driver swerving onto the shoulder. He snuck out all the time, shuffling along the road, feet kicking at the dust and scutch grass. Peter liked to listen to the zither of katydids, watch the blink of fireflies or feel the crunch of snow beneath his feet. The road tonight was clear, the grass dead and limp.

"Thank you for the cloud," Peter said.

Roddy nodded.

"How long will it last?"

"Last?"

"In the globe. Won't it eventually, like, disappear?"

"I don't know. Maybe."

"You've never made one like that before?"

"No."

"Why not?"

"I don't know," Roddy said. "I guess I haven't had a reason to."

Peter took in a deep breath. He felt the light of the stars above. The night was cloudless, and he wondered if, somehow, Roddy wasn't responsible for the dazzling view.

‡

When they reached a curve in the road, Peter sighed and said, "Maybe we should go back. I only usually go this far."

"What's around the bend?" Roddy said.

"More of the same."

"I like it out here. It's quiet."

"It's lonely."

"I guess I could use another beer."

Peter smiled, his teeth like moonlight. Sometimes Roddy liked to imagine that Peter had a gift beyond his prowess in the pool. Maybe his toes were secretly flippers, transforming only when he was in the water, propelling him to victory as if he were a dolphin shimmying along the lane lines. Maybe he could read minds, or make people love him.

They walked shoulder to shoulder. Roddy didn't even have a backyard, much less an expanse of endless land to get lost in, and he felt a small jolt of jealousy. He said so, trying to temper the sentiment with a bark of embarrassing laughter.

"It's not that great," Peter said. "People only ever want to come out here when I have alcohol."

"I was joking about the beer," Roddy said.

"Can I ask you something?" Peter said.

"Anything," Roddy answered, too fast, meaning it.

"What's it like, making the clouds?"

"Oh," Roddy said. He looked down at his hands.

"It's okay," Peter said. "You don't have to explain if you don't want to."

"It's not that. No one's ever really asked."

"Really?"

Roddy shook his head, and Peter nodded.

"I get that, actually. Like, no one really cares about the work that goes into swimming. Did you know I haven't had fried food in, like, years?"

"At least you get to have beer," Roddy said. Peter smiled, but said nothing.

"The stars are nice," Roddy said. He cringed, looking away. He felt stupid, like he couldn't say anything right. All the time, on the bleachers, looking down at Peter, he wanted to be close to him, and now here he was, and Roddy was making himself sound like a moron.

But Peter didn't laugh, or insult him, or say anything at all. He shoved his hands in his pockets and kept walking, taking in a long, deep breath. Roddy tried to do the same, but he was feeling breathless, empty. He stared at his fingers, clenched like claws that he couldn't relax.

‡

We were drunk. Some of us were high. We were cold and tired, even though a fire roared in the firepit, where we made pitstops to improve the circulation in our fingertips. A lot of us were horny. The world was spinning around us, our laughter peals of joy. One girl was crying because her boyfriend broke up with her in the middle of the party, drifting over to join a group of boys who had made a game of standing in a circle and looking down at the ground while one of them threw a heavy stick in the air. The person hit by it had to chug. It was stupid. We were teenagers and we were stupid.

No one had seen Peter or Roddy for a long time. Gage had brought out a tray of Jell-O shots and we were burpy with glucose and vodka. Someone suggested we go on a scavenger hunt for the birthday boy. We called up into the treehouse, but no one called back except for one of the stoners who had failed algebra twice. We marched through the cornfields, screaming Peter's name. Stalks raked our arms, caught our hair. Some of us dropped our beers and didn't bother picking them up. A few of us got lost, trapped in the sameness of the withered vines, and started shrieking until others found us and righted us, brought us back to the dim glow of Peter's house.

And then we tried the yurt.

‡

Peter took Roddy to the yurt.

He had spent next to no time inside, and it smelled vaguely of his brother: Mountain Dew and something rancid, the BO of a kid who hasn't yet figured out that the stink following him around was emanating from his own adolescent armpits.

"Dark in here," Roddy said.

"There's a light. Hang on." Peter rummaged on the ground, felt for the battery-operated lantern his brother kept by the door, and nearly knocked it over with the toe of his shoe. He turned it on, a blast of light that shone over the minimal furnishings: a two-person table, hand-made in the garage, the particle board surface sanded and stained by his brother and father, and a twin-size army cot, the canvas pulled tight.

Roddy sat down. "You come out here a lot?"

Peter shook his head. "My brother. He's into Scouts and stuff. He spends a lot of time here."

"Peaceful."

"It is quiet, I guess."

"You don't like it?"

Peter shrugged. He didn't hate the yurt, but it was a constant reminder of how his parents treated his brother differently: swimming, though it brought Peter popularity, had been an imposition. With Sam, his parents had waited and watched, listening. When Sam asked for a treehouse, his father brought in a contractor to build one. When he wanted to be a Boy Scout, his mother sewed his badges on his sash. When he wanted the yurt, they spent hours researching how best to construct it.

"It's fine," Peter said.

He sat down next to Roddy, who pointed toward the far wall, where Sam had pinned a UGA flag to the wall. "You're going there, right?"

"Yes," Peter said. His father had wanted him to go to Stanford, but his mother hated the idea of him being so far away; she'd rooted for Tennessee or Mizzou. So Peter picked somewhere neither had wanted. The scholarship was massive, and they couldn't come up with a good reason to say no.

"Athens, right? Between the hedges?"

"That's right."

"You'll like it, I bet."

"Have you been there?"

"I've never left Missouri."

"You haven't?"

"My parents can't afford it."

"Oh." Peter sat down next to Roddy, whose hands were in his lap. "What about college?"

"I've applied places." Roddy shrugged. "Mizzou. UMSL. Wash U, but that's a joke."

"Why?"

"Money."

"What about basketball? Or writing?"

Roddy shook his head. "I don't know. It feels like I won't go anywhere."

"What about your clouds?" Peter said.

Roddy held up his hands. "What about them?"

"Dude," Peter said. "You could make so much money."

"How? Being a sideshow freak?"

Peter swallowed a hard breath and felt his cheeks go red. He snatched one of Roddy's hands in his. The skin was smooth, warm. Tiny callouses dotted the base of his fingers.

"People would pay good money for this magic."

Roddy said nothing.

"Maybe you could show me," Peter said, finally. His voice went husky. "You could show me what it's like. Please."

So Roddy did.

‡

The clouds came fast and easy with Peter's hand on Roddy's. The tighter their fingers were intertwined, the quicker they appeared, pluming out like steam.

"Stratus," Roddy whispered.

They filled the yurt, streaming toward the top and settling in cake-like layers. Roddy kept the look in Peter's eyes, the doe-like width of his pupils, the wet warmth directed his way, in mind as he worked. But then Peter looked away, watching the clouds rush out of him. He stood and let go of Roddy, who felt a hard sorrow creep into his chest.

"I've never really felt a cloud before," Peter said. "But I guess you have."

"I have."

Peter pushed his fingers through the thickened air. "It's nice."

Roddy said nothing, watching as Peter spun in a careful pirouette, threading his body through the clouds. His eyes were shut, and Roddy couldn't help but wonder if Peter was imagining himself somewhere else. Perhaps Georgia, strumming through the water, surrounded by cheering fans, in a gargantuan natatorium where Roddy would never be. Maybe at the Olympics in some far away country, or at least the national championships, ready to lead his team to victory. Somewhere distant but within reach, the kind of future that wasn't a flight of fantasy. It wasn't lost in the clouds.

Roddy felt the air thicken into a dense mist. Rain clouds—cumulonimbus—were the heaviest to let go, drawing something deep from his sternum and the tenderness of his heart.

Peter stopped spinning; Roddy could see that he could see, maybe feel, the difference, how the clouds went from wisp to wet, that a new thickness filled the air.

"Roddy?" Peter said.

But then, a rush of cold: the yurt's flap opening. And voices. Lots of them.

‡

When we shoved in through the door, we felt as though we were on a moor in Yorkshire, England. At first we thought it was smoke, that someone was hotboxing. But we couldn't smell that earthy, diesel smell.

Someone at the back of our posse swung the door flap open and shut several times, which helped with ventilation, pulling the strings of fog out into the night where they belonged. Slowly, a picture emerged: Roddy looking down at the scuffed dirt floor, Peter staring at him.

Someone should have said something reassuring. Or even

laughed, or whistled. Anything to break the silence that engulfed the yurt, the only sound the whispered movement of the clouds, tinkling like a cooling engine.

Before we knew it, Roddy was blowing past us, shouldering his way out of the yurt. We turned to give him room to leave. For a while, Peter just stood there, staring, but then he was out into the yard, calling Roddy's name, his voice breaking. He finally stopped following and turned to look at us. We stared at Peter, his broad shoulders slumped, his usually vibrant face scrubbed of joy. All we could see behind his eyes was a storm rolling in. We looked past him, for Roddy, but he was already gone, disappeared into the dark.

YOU CANNOT CONTAIN WHAT'S
BUILT UP INSIDE

The weather is strange here. Six months before the funnel cloud ate up my mother's house, for example, a swamp marched out of the ocean and sucked up the beach, the sand, the towels and umbrellas, a few inattentive sunbathers who didn't realize the mossy muck was getting them before it was too late. The news covered it, reporters and cameramen standing well-away, their eyes worried, harried by nightmares of gators and algae and lily pads leaping up over the levy wall, of cypress trees bursting through the boardwalk and skewering them through their power suits and sports coats. It took three months for all of the Spanish moss and rotting logs to retreat when the shoreline finally fought back, small tidal waves of churning salt water crashing against the swamp and digging in like claws, pulling the muddy bog back into the sea with each rhythmic pulse of the water. People recorded videos, posted them online, and our town became a sensation, a meteorologist's wet dream ("Not like they could have any other kind!" Leno and Conan joked).

Then came the ice storm that killed all of the birds, encasing them in crystalline exoskeletons tinted a summery cerulean. The city had to pay not only to scrape them up off the asphalt (to which they had frozen, as if their icy tombs were adhesive like super glue) but to have new birds transplanted in out of fear that their disappearance would upend the ecosystem; people were terrified by the thought of being overrun by bugs, the ground bursting with worms, all the little vermin that hawks and jays and crows ate growing in number, as though they would rise up in a coup and take over the police station and Walmart and cafes. And no one could forget the rain that melted and dimpled car roofs but left hats and heads untouched. The wind storm that tore off peoples' clothes, plucking away buttons and tearing down zippers as though the air had become so many naughty fingers looking for a glimpse of everyone's unmentionables, but left flyers stapled to telephone poles and sandwich boards standing. Just a week ago an earthquake pulled up the cobblestones in old town's streets but left the interstate on-ramp a few blocks away hearty and smoother than ever.

So the day I walked into my mother's house during the last winter it was still standing, one can understand why I thought hail the size of softballs littered the carpet. Turns out they were just tissues.

‡

The day the boy was murdered my mother was drooped on the living room sofa. The boy's gloves, the reporter on the news was saying, had been stolen. The television panned over footage of the crime scene, showing two uniformed men from the coroner's office guiding the gurney with the boy, snug in a black body bag, into the back of a van from the morgue. The flash of emergency lights was dull in the afternoon sky, which was gray and pixelated. Whether this was an effect of my mother's ancient, tube-back television or the actual sky I couldn't tell. When otherworldly weather was about to start up the air turned all sorts of colors and took on all number of textures: once, when I was a child, before a sandstorm dumped two feet of grit and grain across the yards in our neighborhood, the clouds were a tartan plaid for two days straight, streaky orange like that on a running track darting through the sky. When a dry lightning storm scorched the grass throughout town, the clouds announced it by turning a swirling green color the day before. The Meteorologists—by then there was a whole council of them, housed in a large steel building on the outskirts of town, constantly trying to come up with explanations for the atmospheric misbehavior—scratched their heads and spoke on every local news channel, saying what they always said: we have no idea what to make of this.

My mother let out a plaintive wail and reached for the box of tissues leaning against the couch next to her. I grabbed the remote from the coffee table and shut off the television. I'd already heard about the murder; word of such crimes traveled fast. With the weather out to get us in God-knows-what new ways every day, people tended to leave one another alone. No one could remember the last time someone had been robbed, and even the last reported cases of vandalism—a broken car window, crappy spray paint squiggled across an abandoned building—were but a rusty memory.

But this. A kid.

The air had been colder than usual on the walk to my mother's place, icicles dripping into knife-sharp points and shattering against the sidewalk, leaving divots the size of golf balls. One of them fell against my pea coat and burst as though it was a snowball, leaving a slime of wetness on my right sleeve.

I watched as my mother bunched up a gooey tissue and let it fall to the floor.

"What are you doing?" I said, walking across the room to the window. The blinds were drawn shut so I yanked them up, gloomy half-light eking in and tossing tiny shadows across the floor, dark reflections of the meager, claptrap furniture gathered in the room and the field of wrinkled tissues. I looked at the clouds: still normal, a long sheet of gray. In most parts of the country, the mute pewter was probably depressing or at least disappointing, the kind of gloom that drove people inside to curl up and watch movies while tucked under blankets. For us, the color usually brought relief. Normal, it meant. But perhaps not today. The icicles, the death: it stunk up the driveway and the street and burned through the drains leaking slush into the sewers.

"I can't help but think of your brother," my mother said, wobbly tears in her eyes. "I just want to know if they know who did it, is all. They won't say. Why won't they say?"

I wasn't surprised that she thought of Johnny. Everything reminded her of him, every tragic death, real or fictional. When her favorite TV shows killed off characters, she started talking about him. Ever since he'd been hit by a car that just sped away, leaving him to asphyxiate on the blood that rushed into his punctured lung, every death made my mother see his bruised face, his bleeding nose, his eye already swollen shut. She'd been the first to find him, had been following him out so he could drive her to the grocery store, and he'd forgotten his keys, left them on the drop leaf table next to the door, so she offered to run in and grab them. When she came back out, he was sprawled on the ground by the mailbox, his one open eye glaring up at the clouds as he wheezed, chest heaving like an accordion. The street was empty, and all she'd been able to do was scream *why?* and stare at him while he died, her nose runny, eyes boggled.

It was the last real, brutal crime perpetrated against one person by another in our town.

Until today.

"Why would someone steal that poor boy's gloves?" she said, pulling the beige quilt she'd draped over her body up across her neck, tucking her arms under her chin. She kept staring at the television's black screen, which reflected her face back at her. I had no idea what she was hoping she'd see.

‡

I stayed in my old bedroom that night, only half-asleep, listening for the burp of the television, that electric finger-snap that old sets let out no matter how low the volume was turned last. My mother had a habit of sneaking downstairs and watching the late-night news and infomercials; after Johnny's funeral, she spent a whole week staring at the television through the night no matter how much I objected. Once, she asked if I was really willing to lock my own grieving mother in her bedroom like some kind of prisoner, because that's what it would take for her to let someone else tell her how she should be grieving the fact that her first born had just been murdered. Then she glared at me as though I had committed high treason, some terrible, biting betrayal for which I needed to be punished.

That punishment was nights, on and off for the past five years, of sleeping in my old twin bed, nestled in the corner of my tiny bedroom that overlooked the back yard. Small, with rickety hardwood floors, the room tracked my every step every day of my childhood, announcing to my mother and father every time I might have gotten out of bed after I'd been tucked in. The room was oddly shaped, a square with a narrow jutting extension in the corner, the perfect size for a twin bed. I felt like I was in an open casket when I laid there, and the effect only increased the older I got.

I cooked dinner for my mother the night of the boy's death, standing alone in the kitchen that was way too large for a woman who hated making her own food. She preferred already-prepared meals she could buy at the store: deli sandwiches, dry sausage biscuits, TV dinners, breaded chicken in its various shapes. She paid extra for pre-cut apples, diced pineapple, chicken that had been grilled and stripped and frozen in finger-length segments. She hated cooking pasta, even macaroni and cheese.

"Can we please watch something else, Mom?" I called to her when I heard a newscaster's voice rehashing the story of the dead boy. He'd been strangled, the report said, brutally bruised, his windpipe crushed, his body found in an alley between buildings by a woman taking the trash out from a restaurant after the lunch rush. So far, there were no leads.

"I just want to know if they know what happened to the gloves."

"How would they know that if they don't know who did it?"

"Maybe they found them somewhere."

"Don't you think they'd say so?"

"Don't patronize me, Bainbridge."

"Sorry."

I handed her a plate and sat down next to her on the couch. At least she'd stopped crying and sniffling; the tissues were crowded into a small trash can under the end table.

"Thank you for making dinner."

"I know you don't like to cook."

"It's just, ever since your father—"

"I know, Mom. You don't need to explain."

"I know you worry about me. But you don't need to, Bainbridge."

"Kids worry about their parents, Mom."

"But that's not how it's supposed to go," she said, shaking her head. "We're supposed to worry about you. After children grow up and we have nothing else to look after, we're supposed to get nervous. Think about you. Wonder what you're doing. Hope you'll be okay. Worry." She took a bite, nodded her head to let me know she liked the taste, and swallowed.

"And that's the thing," she said. "I never have to worry about you."

‡

When I was young, maybe seven or eight, the emergency weather announcer interrupted afternoon cartoons to warn that a hurricane was on the way. My mother shut off the television after the bleating announcement was over. It had been accompanied by a whining siren that ached my young ears to the point that I clamped my hands over them and frowned toward my mother. She found my father in his study to tell him about the storm and he went out to nail plywood boards against the front windows. Our living room had a line of them on either side of the front door, with trees close enough that my father feared that the weather might send them crashing through, leaving a splintered rain of glass on the hardwood floor.

Johnny helped, holding a cup of nails in both hands as though he were offering up a glass of communion wine to my father. I stood on the porch and watched. The wind was picking up and the large fronds were slapping against the house with a whipping, rubbery noise. As I watched, I imagined that the wind would knock the rusted ladder over, send my father crashing down to the gravel drive, his bones broken, body bloodied. I was always filled with anxiety whenever my father worked; I pictured the lawnmower escaping his control and running him over, chewing up his feet and spitting out gore-ridden chunks onto the grass in the back yard. Or that, when he changed the car's oil, it would come to life and crush him, squashing down his chest and breaking his ribs, blasting his internal organs out through his abdomen. Nothing happened, of course. Not in the yard, not in the drive, not on the ladder. My father cinched our house up tight and we sat inside, listening to the wind whip, the rain pounding against the walls and roof. Water smacked against the kitchen skylight so hard that I was convinced it would cave in and we'd be washed away. My mother held my hand and smiled.

"It's just a hurricane," she said.

"The regular kind," my father laughed. The year before, the only tropical storm we'd seen had left thousands of dead fish in its wake, sucking them out of the sea and dragging them through the streets. The smell had left people retching for days, the prone fishes' dead eyes staring as people scooped them up by the shovelful and dumped them into plain black trash bags.

‡

In the morning, I woke to my mother calling for the stray cat she leaves food for on the back deck. The porch is screened in, but there's a flap my father cut into the back door when Johnny and I finally wore our parents down with our whining to get a dog. Mom leaves a dish of food out near the door twice a day and sometimes watches from inside for the small tabby to poke its head through the flap and sniff toward the food.

"It's going to snow," she said when she heard my bare feet slapping against the cold hardwood and turned to look at me. "You look exhausted. Didn't you sleep?"

"That bed was comfortable when I was six. Not so much anymore. How do you know?"

"You've got dark circles under your eyes. A mother always knows."

"I mean about the snow."

"You can smell it out here. Like ash, but without the burning sensation in your nostrils."

I stepped onto the porch where the floor was even colder despite the thin felt carpet that my father had laid down over the cement more than twenty years ago. Through the space between the roof and the trees that lined the back of the yard, I could see a gloomy blank slate in the sky.

"You know that cat's never going to leave, right?"

"Why would I want it to?"

"It's a stray."

"I call him Boots. He's got white feet and black everywhere else."

I yawned and shivered. "I have to go to work. Are you okay?"

Instead of answering, my mother rattled the dish full of dry food and called for the cat, stretching out the vowel in Boots as though she were yodeling. She set down the bowl and looked out into the yard. I watched her head turn ever so slowly, scanning the grass and the base of the shrubs and trees.

"You know," I said, "you could always catch the cat and keep it here. If you want a pet so bad."

"I don't need a pet," she said, turning to me. "I just like having someone to take care of now and then, you know?"

I nodded.

My mother smiled and walked inside, stopping to give me a kiss on the cheek. "You should shower. I'm going to see if there's any news about the boy and his gloves. I just wonder about the gloves. Really, what could someone want with them?"

‡

The police got a break three days later, but no one knew about it because the snowstorm my mother predicted did hit. What she didn't predict was that it would knock out everyone's electricity. My mother was at the library at the time of the discovery, I calculated, where she volunteered shelving books three days a week in the afternoon to keep herself busy. I'd suggested she not go in that day considering the impending storm, but she had to, she told me, because otherwise she would sit at home and think about the dead boy, and that would make her think about Johnny, and then she'd worry about me for God knows what reason, and then Boots, and even if she tried to read a book or watch something besides the news her mind would wander and she'd end up turning off the television or put down her magazine and just stare into space while the clock on the wall ticked off minute after minute.

I was late to pick her up because of the thick swirls of snow, which she watched from the relative safety of the library, an old brick building that had managed to somehow find itself immune from the weather for as long as anyone could remember. "Who knows," she said afterward, waving away my apologies for not getting her sooner, "what else that horrid snow might have done. Besides, it was warm in there. You'd be surprised what kind of heat books can give off."

We lit candles—"Not too many, and don't set them so close to the wallpaper; you know they'll leave soot marks, which give me the willies," my mother said—and sat in the pale gloom of early evening. When I asked if she was hungry and she gave me a nonchalant shrug, it meant yes, she was hungry, but I shouldn't concern myself on her account, I went into the kitchen and looked through the pantry and found only a bag of potato chips, which we ate in relative silence, my mother apologizing for not having more to offer without having to open up the refrigerator and let the food spoil.

I stayed the night again because the snow was piling up in heaps, plus my mother refused to let me drive home, her voice nearly breaking when she begged me to stay, apologizing for the uncomfortable bed in my room, and would I prefer to sleep in hers? When I said no, she looked me in the eyes and said thank you.

"For what?"

"Being all a mother could want or need."

I wasn't sure what to say, so I said good night and went upstairs, floorboards creaking beneath my feet. I wondered, as I brushed my teeth, how my mother would occupy herself in the mausoleum that was our house during such a storm. She had nowhere to escape to, no television to divert her gaze, no stray cat dredging through the murky snow to keep her company. Boots was out there somewhere, I thought as I lay on my side and stared at the trees and grass and everything else pummeled by inch after inch of snow. That cat, navigating its way through the weather without a roof over its head. How it had survived so long in this town I had no idea.

The power snapped back on early in the morning, a buzz fizzing throughout the house as the television kicked back on—Mom must have left it on when she left for the library, "So I could have the sound of a voice when I came home," she said—and alarm clocks flashed 12:00. I heard the whisper of the news from downstairs, then my mother yelling my name.

"They found something, Bainbridge!" she said when I came downstairs. She was sitting on the edge of the couch, staring at the TV set, eyes watery. "Oh, it's *awful*."

"What is it?"

Before she spoke, my mother broke her gaze on the television and stared at me. The look on her face shook me, and I grew so cold all of a sudden that I had to look around to make sure a window wasn't open or that snow hadn't barreled through the front door, or that frost hadn't started circling the house in some vicious wrapping paper. No, it was just my mother, staring at me with opaque, lost eyes.

"Mom?"

"Another boy. It was another boy. He didn't have gloves and he wanted some. Oh, God. Oh, God. So he just took them. Killed that boy and left him there. For gloves. Nothing but gloves."

‡

My father had a heart attack while making dinner one night when I was eleven. I was home alone with him; Mom had just gone out to pick up Johnny from his first high school basketball practice, and I was sitting at the kitchen table watching my father slice zucchini. He, unlike my mother, was a firm believer in preparing one's own meals. During the week, he got up early before work and made massive sandwiches on artisan breads with fresh lettuce and tomatoes and stuffed them in brown paper bags for me and Johnny, and I would amble downstairs well before my brother and mother just to watch my father's work. He would often fake a heart attack, pretending I'd terrified him to death when I snuck into the kitchen. I watched his shoulders shake as he sliced tomatoes and cut off the crusts of my sandwiches, acting as if he didn't know I was there. Eventually it became a game: me, trying to be as quiet as possible, my father turning at just the right moment, catching me off-guard, pretending to die of fright at seeing me. His fake surprise was meant to surprise me.

So when a weird look came over my father, as though he smelled something not quite rancid so much as out of place, and he reached up toward his left arm with the large knife still in his right, I thought he was joking. I started laughing. I remember that the sound of my giggling was high, unabashedly so for a boy on the cusp of puberty, bouncing off the steel appliances and marbled backsplash. My father looked at me and tried to crack a smile even as he grimaced and choked out a "No" and fell down, the knife clattering on the tile floor. Even then I thought it was a ruse, my father taking our charade to a new place, adding another element because we needed something more. When he didn't get up I started to feel a fluttering panic in my stomach, a sensation I'd never experienced before, and the lightheadedness that accompanied my inability to shake my father back to himself, back to life, sucked out all of the emergency procedures my parents had ever taught me. I forgot to dial 911. I forgot to run to the neighbor's house across the street. I almost forgot to breathe. I cried and waited, holding my father's t-shirt, tugging at the fabric as though moving him even a little bit would wake him up.

Mom found us entangled on the kitchen floor, alerted by my sobs that something was wrong. Johnny stood behind her as she ran into the kitchen and shrieked, yelling over her shoulder for him to call 911 once she sorted out that I hadn't. She pushed me aside with a gruffness that I've never forgotten, a hardness in her hand that coursed through my shoulder. And then she was immediately tender with my father, stroking his cheek with her finger as though he were a delicate glass statue that might shatter under the weight of her nails. She stared at him and I stared at her staring at him, and then Johnny spoke up.

"The ambulance is on the way, Mom," he said. "Mom, is he going to be okay? Is Dad going to be okay?"

My mother said nothing, just kept staring. Ten years later, I would see that stare again as I sat next to my mother at my brother's funeral, her eyes set against his prone face, peaceful in the lined interior of his coffin. The look never left her, haunting her gaze like a tattoo inked behind her pupils.

‡

It wasn't long before the funnel cloud came, a swirling mass of tree branches, leaves, demolished birds' nests. This time, though, it wasn't isolated to our coastal town; the National Weather Service followed it as it stormed up Florida, tickling in toward the Carolinas, newscasters wondering where it would go, what it would do. How it would slow down. We knew that it would only dissipate once it found us, that such a strange, uncanny thing could only belong to our town, that it was coming to us to release all of its pent up destruction. But I knew that it wasn't for the town but my mother and me, that this funnel cloud was here to tear up our house; everything else was just collateral.

That day, the funnel first lumbered through the outskirts of town, giving me enough time to cut out of work early and race to my mother's house. We already knew that the cloud was plucking up houses, ripping them from their foundations and sucking up walls, sinks, beds, leaving the inhabitants unharmed, standing where their bathrooms and hallways once were, surrounded by nothing but concrete foundations and the few possessions they managed to cling to hard enough that they wouldn't be gobbled up by the swirling mass. Later, survivors would describe the experience as being kissed by cotton, wrapped up in a confusing, comforting blanket, warm as a womb.

"Like I was safe. It was almost heavenly, but in a slimy, disorienting way," one woman would say, grimacing.

My mother was lying on the couch, staring at the television with the volume too low for me to make out what was being said. She'd been like that since the police reported that another boy, only a year or two older than the dead child, had wanted the missing gloves badly enough that he tried to take them and the boy wouldn't give them, so a fight ensued, the killer unable to hold in his rage at his victim's obstinance and so he lashed out, the fight ending with the one strangling the other and taking the gloves. This news had broken my mother, all of the tied up sorrow and anxiety spilling out of her, bursting her like she was a water balloon, and she seeped into the couch and spent her days there. She didn't leave the house, didn't sleep in her bed, didn't ask me to stay any more. Told me to leave if my tone of voice displeased her.

"Mom," I said, "we should get out of here. The storm is coming."

She said nothing; it was like I wasn't even there.

"Mom. This house is going to go. The storm's coming right for us. It'll rip the house apart."

"I'll be okay," she murmured.

"Mom."

She sat up. "Bainbridge."

The look on her face felt like the biting, brusque grip she'd had on my shoulder when my father died and she pushed me away. A cold, hard casing wrapping around her and shutting me out like the birds that had been entombed in their icy bodices. I told her I loved her, to which she said nothing, and I turned around, left the house, shut the door. I stood across the street; I could see the massive funnel cloud, shingles and window panes and carpeting swirling around above rooftops, not far away. I sat in the grass and waited.

The final look on my mother's face told me she would not come out of the house. And I knew that, when the storm came, my mother would rise up with her things. I would watch and pray for my mother's happiness, letting all my worry for her drift up too, carry her to wherever she would go. I hoped that, among those leaves and armchairs, she would find what she needed. I knew she would go, drift away into the air and beyond, because she could no longer stand on the ground where everything she knew had been broken.

A MILLION HEARTS CAN'T ALL BE BROKEN

The morning after the date, Harold peels back the sheets and looks at his stomach, where the muscles are stretched and bloated. When he touches his skin, he can feel a second heartbeat working in fast syncopation beneath his regular pulse: a second heart.

He checks his phone: no message from Ray, no response to his thanks for the good time. Of course, he sent it late—eleven-thirty—and woke early—seven-fifteen—so it's entirely possible that Ray hasn't seen it yet. But Ray had admitted that he was a night owl, an idiot who liked to drink coffee at midnight. Harold had nodded at this, managed to hold back that he was a morning person who rarely consumed caffeine except in certain teas, side-stepping the subject by asking what Ray did when he was up late.

"Not much," Ray said. "I write poems sometimes."

"I'd love to read one."

Rather than demurring, Ray smiled and said, "I'll email you one." But then he hadn't.

Harold lays with his hands pressed against the sides of his belly until he's familiar with the rhythm of this new heart. Last time, with Anya, the heart had grown in his left calf, pressed against his fibula, which had made his morning runs a challenge, more an issue of comfort than practicality. He'd also struggled to put on his compression sleeves, which kept his knees from getting inflamed and angry. That heart had been like a whale's, barely reaching thirty beats per minute. This new one flares with such speed that he can't even begin to count its rate. He's not sure what the difference might mean.

Harold stands, blood rushing from his head, leaving his vision splotchy with purple and yellow. He gathers himself, takes a breath, and then walks to the bathroom where he stares into the mirror. Harold looks vaguely pregnant, like one of those stick-thin models with a melon-sized baby bump even at six, seven, whatever months. Who knows? Not Harold, that's for sure. He's made it clear to everyone he's ever been with, early on, that he isn't interested in kids. He said so to Anya on their first date, and her response was to lift her wine glass and clink it against his. And yet, eight months in, she shifted course, saying, "People change, Harold," to which he said, "But I haven't." They couldn't decide who was being unfair. Maybe, Harold thinks, they both were. Or neither. That night, the heart in his leg wilted, vanishing into his bloodstream. The next day he hardly had to say a word to Anya. She looked at the bulge of his corduroys—or the lack thereof—and knew. Her own second heart, located next to her first, was still there, she said, though it was squeezed behind her sternum, so Harold had never actually seen it. Maybe something was ending that hadn't actually started. Anya left, taking her cosmetics bag and the small stack of panties that had occupied half of his underwear drawer with her. She left behind her smell, lemon verbena, and a toothbrush cantilevered next to his in an aquamarine coffee cup.

He still has the toothbrush, though the bristles have gone hard. He plucks it from the mug and feels them, rough like a beard against his fingertips. At the end of their date, he and Ray stood outside the restaurant, both toeing their shoes through the loose pebbles of the parking lot. Ray chose the place, a low-lit gastropub with good wheat beers and sliders, a tray of which they'd shared, Ray leaning over the table at one point to wipe a smear of spicy garlic aioli from the edge of Harold's mouth.

Harold didn't want the date to end, but he had no idea what to say to keep it going. Suggest a nightcap? Offer a walk around the reinvigorated business district that surrounded them? Fortunately, Ray made the move, putting his hands on Harold's shoulders, then leaning in and kissing him, soft, his lips tasting of salt and sesame and yeast, a pleasant combination that reminded Harold of going to a baseball game. He opened his mouth and Ray's tongue made a slide toward his teeth. When Ray backed away, Harold smiled. And then they parted without a word.

Harold waves the toothbrush like a wand, aimed toward his reflection. He laughs at himself, then prods at the heart anchoring his stomach. When he pokes at the skin with the toothbrush, he can feel the heart, its ventricles and atria filling and emptying in rapid motion. He throws the toothbrush in the trash.

He decides to run. Harold isn't fast, nor does he go very far—his longest run in the last year is four miles—but he enjoys the park near his house, a sprawling array of gazebos and frog ponds and running paths that cross over one another like the US interstate system. The tree coverage is good on hot, sunny days like this one, gargantuan oaks extending their branches over the paths. Harold enjoys taking in the visible hearts of strangers, his stares shielded by his sunglasses. He sees mothers with two or three extra hearts pulsing from their shoulders or hips or quads, one for each of their children. Two shirtless men ambling side by side, clearly identical twins with the same pursed Cupid's bow lips and sharp jawlines, have nearly-matching hearts protruding from their left obliques, the pulses matching their strides: love for one another, Harold imagines. An elderly couple wearing matching plum pantsuits that reveal the outlines of hearts bursting from their backs—his at his coccyx, hers at her right scapula—sits down on a bench near a drinking fountain, both of them leaning forward. Harold imagines a life bent like that is easier when you have someone who curves with you.

And then, he knows, there are the hearts he can't see: tiny hearts embedded deep in the cerebellum, or the gluteus maximus, or ribcage, small enough to avoid detection by the outside world. He wonders about people with those hearts, if they feel pressure to talk about them, to prove their love. Do they ask their husbands and wives and girlfriends and children to probe at them with fingertips, to press their ears close and listen for the extra beats? What is it like to have to amplify your love, to drum up proof?

As he's finishing his final mile and slowing to a walk, his phone, strapped to his left arm, vibrates. Harold is fast to rip it from its case, his fingers leaving oily streaks as he unlocks the screen. Though he's tired and his pulse already beats fast, his hearts, both, uptick when he sees the message is from Ray.

‡

Ray finishes showering and finds his roommate Ryan has made a feast of a brunch, though for Ryan "made" really means bought: croissants from the bakery below their apartment, a fruit tray from the boutique grocery, prosciutto rolls and charcuterie from the delicatessen where his boyfriend Javier works, orange juice that Ryan will pretend is fresh-squeezed, and a bottle of Andre champagne in a marble cooling sleeve.

When Ray tries to sit, Ryan holds out a hand like a crossing guard. He brushes hair from his face—they've argued about whether Ryan needs a haircut—and says, "Not so fast. You only get to eat if you spill."

Ray rolls his eyes but nods.

"Thank god. I'm starving." Ryan throws himself down at the table and gnaws on a croissant. When he swallows, the little heart embedded in his neck pulses with extra speed. It first appeared two weeks after Ryan and Javier started dating. He threw open Ray's bedroom door, not worried or caring that Ray was naked under his top sheet, to show him. Ray had nodded in approval. It is the largest of dozens, maybe hundreds, of hearts that dot Ryan's shoulders and arms, ranging in size from ping pong balls to peas, studding him like he's coated in cancer or sebaceous cysts. They beat in a singular, steady rhythm, pulsing like Ryan is a subwoofer letting out a silent heavy bass. Ray knows one of those many humped hearts is for him, not because he and Ryan have ever been romantically involved, but because of the many kinds of love Ryan has to offer.

"So," Ryan says through a mouthful of buttery dough. "What are you thinking?"

Ray plucks up the champagne and uncorks it, bubbly liquid purling down the side of the bottle. He fills a pair of flutes, handing one to Ryan, who takes a careful sip and then sets the glass to the side, doming his fingers in front of him. "Don't try to distract me with day drinking." "It was good," Ray says.

"You sound like you're talking about a doctor's visit."

"He was lovely."

"You got home late."

Ray laughs. "It was ten-thirty."

"Late for a first date."

"Nothing happened. Or, well, I guess we kissed."

"Who kissed who?"

"It couldn't be mutual?"

Now Ryan laughs. "Not on the first date."

"I kissed him."

"Hmm." Ryan scans him. Ray knows that he's looking for a heart. But there isn't one to be found, visible or otherwise. Ray's last boyfriend, a medical student who liked to play doctor in bed, was constantly on the prowl, searching for signs of another heart; ultimately, five months in, when he had already sprouted a second one along his left forearm, squashed between his ulna and radius, the lack of another heart anywhere in Ray had ended the relationship.

"I need," the med student had said as he left, "someone who loves me as much as I love them."

Ray had wanted to say it wasn't a competition, but he'd let him go. Many times before, he had felt the kind of scrutiny that the medical student subjected him to, even in the aftermath of a one-night stand, when he and a relative stranger lay stretched out on a top sheet or tangled at odd angles on a living room sofa. Despite the tacit agreement that their encounter was meant for quick, salty satisfaction, he was constantly aware of the way his hookups would scan his body, questions poised on pursed lips or hovering behind slitted eyes. How, they were asking without asking, could there be no marks of love?

Ryan finishes his glass of champagne and refills both of their flutes. "So what are you going to do now?"

"I don't know."

Ryan sighs. "You know, it doesn't have to be love at first sight."

"What if it's not love at all?"

"Could be that, too. Is there any harm in another date?"

"I guess not."

"Invite him to Javier's meat and cheese tasting. I can scope him out."

"Okay. Sure."

Ryan nods. His arms seem to blur as he eats. The one heart that beats out of rhythm is the one on his neck, the one for Javier. Ray imagines what it feels like to have so many, or even just more than one. When he's jogging, or having sex, or climbing too many stairs in one go, or doing more squats than his legs want him to, he finds himself listening to the singular beat of his solitary heart, how clear and pristine the noise is, but then he sees those around him with their extras, and he curdles a little bit at the symphony that everyone but him can hear.

‡

Javier's eyebrow piercing catches the sun coming in through the windows and sends a dancing beam up against the ceiling. He follows it, bobbing his head so it flitters to the music pumping from the shop's speakers. The deli is, for all intents and purposes, his, the owner, Melanie, currently experiencing a mid-life crisis mixed with a windfall from the recent death of her octogenarian third husband, whose life insurance policy is funding a cross-country trip that has left Javier to himself. She's somewhere in Colorado right now, probably flirting with sexy, young ski instructors while she pretends stupidity and takes to the bunny slopes. She never checks in, has basically given him full control, with a generous pay increase to go along with the added responsibilities. She still pays the rent, and he still deposits the profits into her business account after going over the books every Sunday night, and when the margins are solid she floats him a bonus, a personal transaction through PayPal so he doesn't have to report any of it in taxes. "A gift," she's called it, practically winking into the phone.

When Ryan arrives with Ray and Harold in tow, three couples are already in the deli, each armed with paper plates heaped with sliced meats and cheeses, and the three additional bodies make the place feel like a packed club. The deli is on the corner of a long, glass-encased strip mall, next to a dentist's office and a Chinese restaurant and twenty-four hour gym. A single booth is stuffed between the door to the customer bathroom slash janitorial closet and a vending machine stocked with Coke products. Three round two-top tables, which Javier salvaged from a Greek restaurant across the street when it went under six months ago, stud the wall of windows and serve as the deli's only other seating. They rarely see use; people only really sit down on the random weekends when Javier chooses to make in-house paninis with bread he buys at the bakery and he sets a chalkboard outside on the curb, announcing the sandwiches as a lunch special.

The first thing Javier notices is the bulge at Harold's stomach. Harold, who he's never met. Harold, who is handsome in a wind-swept way, narrow in the shoulders and hips, his exposed calves showing off that he is definitely a runner; the weird convex shape of his stomach can only mean one thing.

More than once Javier has had to reassure Ryan that when he told him he loved him—which came fast, only a month into their relationship—he meant it, even though he couldn't prove it. He and Ryan are exact opposites: where Ryan's tiny hearts bleed up into his arms for everyone to see, Javier's, though present, stay buried deep. The moment he knew he loved Ryan he had felt the heart emerge in his left lung, which made him feel queasy and constricted, as if someone was holding him in a tight bear hug. He supposes that is as appropriate a feeling for the first crashes of love as any.

All his life he's had to defend the closeness of his hearts, how they bury themselves deep down, often tangled somewhere in the thickness of his intestines, hidden behind viscera and organs, unlike Harold's obvious bulge. Javier glances at Ray, wondering if he's shown any signs. He wishes he could have seen Ray's face when he first saw the heart pulsing underneath Harold's white chambray shirt, the fabric of which flutters with its quick pulse.

"Hey," Ryan says. He doesn't try to lean over the meat counter and kiss Javier, instead laying a palm atop the glass that Javier pokes with his index finger. Javier likes this gestural intimacy, and it makes the heart in his lung beat with extra strength. Ray nods at him and introduces Harold, whose hand he shakes. Javier has set up the charcuterie and some fruit on the low slab of countertop where he usually weighs cuts of beef and pork. He tells them to help themselves, take however much they want; he can always slice and dice more. Ryan nods, winks, and hands out plates.

Javier watches them plunk pepper jack and pepperoni in their mouths. When one of the couples that had taken up space at the low tables leaves, Ryan hustles Ray and Harold over to the empty seats while Javier helps a woman pick out ribeyes for the anniversary dinner she is prepping for her husband, whom she clearly still loves if the heart beating behind her left ear is any indication (unless, Javier thinks, she has fallen out of love with him and in love with someone else). When the woman leaves, butcher-papered meat clung tight to her chest as if she thinks someone might steal it before she reaches her car, Ryan comes up and leans across the glass, whispering, "I think it's going well."

"I think they can hear you," Javier says.

"I'm talking about your tasting."

"Oh. Thanks."

Javier can smell the spices on Ryan's breath. The heart in his throat is throbbing. Javier is glad for this barometer of Ryan's feelings, this dowsing rod he can use to navigate toward the things that make his boyfriend happiest. When Javier reaches out and cuffs Ryan's forearm he can see the heart pick up speed. He wishes he could give Ryan such a sign beyond verbal assurances, because while voices can lie, other parts of the body cannot. He always tells Ryan when the heart in his lung is crushing his breath, but Javier is never sure Ryan believes him.

"I was thinking," Javier says, "that I could close up early today."

Ryan grins at him, waggling his eyebrows. "Look at you being saucy."

"Well, I've been working hard here, and you've been working hard there." Javier nods toward Ray and Harold, who are laughing about something, their voices low, heads bent toward one another in faux-secrecy.

"They seem happy, don't they?" Ryan says. He drops his voice. "It's sometimes hard to tell. You know."

Javier nods. He releases Ryan's arm as a trio of young men come barging through the door; he recognizes one of them, a guy who comes around every few weeks for black forest ham. Ryan moves away from the counter as the men homing missile toward the free food, which Javier needs to replenish. He looks them over: no obvious hearts bulging from their torsos or hips or legs, but that doesn't mean much. Javier glances over at Ryan, who is leaning over Ray and Harold, the outline of his spine visible through his t-shirt. Things can be hidden away easily, Javier thinks.

‡

Harold takes a sip of the spicy red wine in his glass then leans his head back, the squeaky leather of the sofa groaning beneath his weight. Ryan sits across from him on an identical love seat, drinking from his own glass, but he doesn't say anything. Javier and Ray are mumbling at one another in the kitchen. The apartment smells of roast beef sizzling under the broiler. The heart in Harold's abdomen pulses. One of Ryan's arms is propped on the back of the couch, his skin warbling with motion. The sight is dizzying, like a tiny, silent orchestra. Harold wonders what it's like for Ryan to hear and feel so much.

When Ray invited Harold over for a double date, he could hardly say yes fast enough; the heart in his gut started gonging like he was being punched. It sent a quake of pleasant nausea up his throat. This, now, is their sixth or seventh date, the most intimate; following the tasting, there was miniature golf, a movie, an afternoon picnic where they both drank too many canned IPAs Ray had brought along in a tiny cooler. But they have done no more than kiss. These, at least, have hardly been chaste; after enough beer was in his system, Ray's mouth went slack and wet, and he clung to Harold for a long time. Harold didn't usually go in for public displays, but his body was yearning, hungry.

Javier steps into the living room with a tray of appetizers, bruschetta piled with diced tomato and a balsamic drizzle; the pungent aroma of garlic nabs at Harold's jaw. Ryan leans forward and grabs a piece, the bread crunching between his teeth.

"Amazing," he says, smiling up at Javier. His largest heart flutters.

Harold has told himself to be patient. Every time he sees Ray, he has not changed in any noticeable way, no curved mass visible anywhere on his body. Harold tries not to stare, to be too searing in the inquisition of his eyes, but he cannot help himself.

Ray finally joins them, filling their glasses with the last of the bottle and uncorking a second, which he sets on the coffee table. The label is covered in salamanders and cartoonish hearts. *Hearts Burn*, it's called, a name that Harold doesn't think can possibly do it any marketing favors. Harold, who teaches ninth and tenth grade history, asks his students every year on Valentine's Day if they know why hearts are drawn in a shape that doesn't resemble the real thing in any way, and none of them know. This leads into a long exegesis he's given more times than he can count about how it's a trick question, really, as no one is quite certain of how we ended up with the pointed lower tip, the two bulging arches (the red, of course, is easy to explain: blood and love and warmth, etcetera). He tells them about pottery from 3000 BCE first identified as symbolic of the heart but more likely a representation of fig leaves or ivy; then there's the proposal that the ancient extinct plant silphium inspired the shape. It was used as birth control and the town of Cyrene put its shape on their money because of how lucrative its trade was. He mentions the *Roman de la poire*, in which a man hands his heart to his lover, the organ's shape likened to a conifer cone. A similar symbol appears on the thirteenth century royal banner of the kings of Denmark.

Harold could go on and on. So many hearts.

Ray smells of beef stock and beachy cologne. His shoulders are angled toward Harold's. He and Ryan and Javier talk, Harold listening and drinking, smiling when appropriate. A buzzer goes off in the kitchen, and Javier and Ray depart again, Ryan calling out something about a third bottle of wine. He and Harold sit in chummy silence, Ryan squinting, his eyes already laced with the veneer of drink. The sun has started to set, and the ambient lighting is low, as if they are at a bistro in Paris. Harold feels content, and the heart in his stomach flutters, its beat fast and powerful. When Ray calls out that dinner is served, he feels the pulse all through him, an endless wave of pleasant shocks.

At the end of the night, when Javier and Ryan have vanished, their wineglasses cleaned out and upended on a drying rack, Harold pulls on his jacket, but then, at the last second, as he's about to step out the door, Ray cuffs his arm, his grip tight. Harold wonders if he can feel the dual beats of his heart through the leather. Ray looks him in the eye and simply says, "Stay?" and of course Harold does.

‡

When he was a teenager, Ray watched his classmates fall in love, their bodies bursting with new hearts that would shrivel and disappear just as fast as they bloomed. This was young love, a kind of lust-attraction that his peers couldn't distinguish from the real thing. And even though he felt the same kind of hormone-driven desire for his classmates—dreams about the quarterback of the football team and the head cheerleader took turns leaving him with throbbing erections when he woke in the middle of the night, upper lip sweaty, pillowcase damp—his body was always its same smooth, endless self. To make up for it, he learned how to say the word love in a dozen languages: *amor, agape, ljubezen, dragoste, die liebe, rakkaus, armastus, liefde*. He would whisper the word to himself in foreign tongues, convinced that if the right combination of sounds came from his lips his body would co-operate. His first girlfriend examined him after they had sex for the first time, her own fresh heart a lump anchoring the bottom of her left breast. When she could find nothing she cried.

Ray wakes to the hot presence of Harold's bulk. Harold is still asleep, rolled onto his right side. He has a nice back, the wavy curvature of his spine a series of tiny morse code blips surrounded by crunchy muscle. Ray looks himself over, raising the sheet, but all he sees is his normal torso and legs and crotch. He lets out a short sigh. Harold stirs and turns toward him. He's good, Harold, about keeping his gaze steady, careful to only glance over Ray's body when he thinks Ray isn't looking.

But Ray is better. He can see the way Harold's eyes keen with hope as they search Ray's chest and thighs, how he waits until Ray swings out of bed and pads to the bathroom to check his lower back, his feet. Ray closes the bathroom door behind him and lets out a long breath. Leaning against the vanity, he stares at himself; nothing on his neck or behind his ears or the back of his skull. But he knows that. He would feel a second heartbeat, clear and clamorous. But inside all is silent aside from the single slow thud that has always been there.

‡

Javier looks up from the meat slicer and is surprised to see Harold. It takes him a second to place him, only because he's only seen Harold with the bulge above his waistline, but now he's trim and slim, all evidence of his second heart gone.

The deli is empty, a mid-afternoon lull. He's been cleaning, and the windows sparkle with sunlight and the last pesky streaks of cleaner that he can never quite polish away. Instead of the usual slight offal smell, the deli is tinged with bleach and sanitizer.

"Hi," Javier says. "Good to see you."

"Thanks," Harold says.

"I didn't know you lived around here."

Harold shrugs. "I was in the neighborhood. Thought I'd support local business."

"Anything you need in particular?"

"I'm having some people over. What steaks do you recommend?"

Javier eyes Harold. The tragic thing about hearts is that when they're broken, there's no evidence. They simply vanish, curling up into nothing. He can tell he should say something about Ray, that this is what Harold really wants, but instead he gives his basic spiel: ribeyes are the fattiest and thus have lots of flavor; strip steaks are easy to cook and have a nice chew to them; hanger steaks are great for marinating if you're into that; short ribs can be unexpectedly fun and tender with the right sauce, and no, they don't have to always be braised.

He stops: Harold isn't listening. His gaze is both close and far away.

"I just wish I knew what I did wrong," he says.

"Oh," Javier says.

"Have you ever wondered that?"

"All the time. I think everyone does."

Harold shakes his head. "Sorry. I shouldn't be unloading on you."

Javier takes a deep breath. He tugs off his apron, which reeks of streaky fat and protein. He walks around the counter. Harold doesn't say a word and doesn't move away when Javier embraces him. They're about the same height, the same build. They fit together. Harold smells of some brut cologne he's applied too liberally at his throat, but the tingle in Javier's nostrils is nice. He thinks he should say something about heartbreak, about the hidden depths of love and sorrow, but then Harold wraps his arms around Javier and lets out a small groan that Javier recognizes as a release, a latch that he's finally let open. Javier latches his fingers together, feeling the engagement ring that Ryan presented the night before, kneeling down on his apartment floor while they watched trashy television and drank prosecco. Javier said yes, felt the leap of his second heart deep inside him. Ryan, afterward, laid his head on Javier's chest and laughed, saying, "I can hear it! I can hear it."

And right now, Javier hears it too. He also hears Harold's heart, the singular thudding in his chest, synchronizing with Javier's pair. They both close their eyes and listen, each of them hearing a different song.

UPON A CUTTING

When Connie first cut herself, drawing our father's straight razor along the tender inside of her left thigh, her blood sang. It was not the hymnal song of a fat lip or papercut, nor the popstar sound of a bloody nose, or the whale song of menstruation. Her blood let loose the gravel-growl of a smoker, the babble of Kurt Cobain or Eddie Vedder. My stomach twisted when the sound burst through my bedroom door, a horrible, incomprehensible language.

By the time I looked into the hallway, my parents were already at the bathroom door. My mom had been preparing dinner, a spicy beef and lentil stew; the smell of shallots and garlic and rich dry wine had slithered beneath my doorjamb and set my stomach growling, but at the onset of the singing my appetite vanished. Dad looked disheveled, having fallen asleep on his recliner after a long day at work.

Mom was pounding on the door, demanding that Connie open up. I could tell that my sister had made a second cut because the singing grew louder, twin voices gargling out the same strangled lyrics but in a round, the voice of the second cut not quite catching up with the first. Mom's yelling was swallowed by the horrible singing, but I could hear her desperation as she slammed her fists against the door. Dad glanced at me but didn't say anything. His eyes were owlish, his shoulders curled inward, his hands flat steaks at his sides. When I was seven years old, he suffered a compound fracture to his right leg during an adult soccer game. The wound screamed like the lead singer in a hair band, the high-octave howl matching my father's. It took twenty minutes for an ambulance to arrive, and by the time the EMTs appeared, my father had stopped shrieking but his wound had not. The noise echoed in my ears for days. Listening to the singing of my sister's self-inflicted hurt, I knew it was a sound I would never forget.

‡

A week before Connie cut herself, I lost my virginity. Nicholas came up to me Thursday afternoon while I was weighing down my backpack with my AP textbooks and whispered, "I'm ready. Tomorrow?" My cheeks flared with so much blood I thought they might sing.

We went to his house on Friday afternoon because his parents were out of town. He took my hand as soon as he answered the door, as if he thought I might fly away or change my mind, and led me down a hallway to the bedrooms, away from the dizzying scent of his mother's potted jasmine and spearmint. He shut his bedroom door behind us even though we were alone, and then, without a word, he started undressing. I scrambled to keep up.

By some unspoken agreement, we arranged ourselves: him on his back on the bed, me standing before him. He pulled a bottle of lube from his nightstand, and when I asked about condoms, he looked up at me through the dark frazzle of his hair and said, "Have you done this with anyone else?" When I shook my head no, he handed me the bottle, which was heavy and cold. I poured a quarter-size dob of liquid into my palm, where it wobbled like a jelly. As I stroked myself, Nicholas stared up at the ceiling. His parents had taken him to the Gulf Shores for spring break and he still had his tan. His body was lithe and sinewy from playing varsity tennis, a pale outline of his athletic shorts lighting up his crotch, like a spotlight was beaming down on his genitals. When I was finished with the lube, he took the bottle and, without looking at himself, applied a smear.

"Don't worry," he said. "I didn't eat lunch." He told me he'd watched videos on how to prepare. He'd even laid a towel beneath his hips.

My tongue was thick, every part of my mouth sucked dry.

"Okay," he said with a long exhale. He lifted his knees. I clutched his right ankle, the skin smooth, bone strong in my palm. Then, guiding myself with my free hand, I pushed inside him.

Despite my attempt to be slow and careful, and despite the lake of lube we'd used, I heard the singing immediately, a whispered aria. Nicholas had his eyes closed, lids pinched at the edges. His mouth was a tight knot of flesh, chin pointing at the ceiling. His throat was pulled taut, Adam's apple a rising crag that buoyed and shifted as he swallowed. I moved in and out and he nodded, conveying nothing. The singing grew louder.

"Keep going," he said, though I hadn't stopped. My body was filled with a thrumming tension, cool numbness swirling toward my center. Nicholas reached out a hand and tugged at my hip, pulling me into him deeper. Tightness washed over me, and the singing—a woman's voice, rich and deep and vibrating—increased. Blood and heat centered in my groin, and soon I was collapsed over him, spent. Even though it had been quick, my body percolated with sweat. Nicholas laid a hand on my back.

"Wow," he said.

We were both a sticky mess. Something ticked in my head like I was a car engine popping and cooling. Nicholas kissed my neck. If he was upset that he hadn't come, he didn't show it. He held me tighter. We were both silent as the singing continued. I was too close to him to see the look on his face, but his throat was still elongated. He smelled of salt. I pressed my mouth to his ear, ready to whisper something, but I'd lost my voice. It pained me that the singing of his blood was the only sound.

‡

Connie was the most popular freshman in school. She was an actor and singer, stealing the leading role of Emily in *Our*

Town from a senior who'd been waiting for years to take the spotlight in the fall play. She did the same when it came time for the spring musical, a break from our school's long tradition of only granting upperclassmen those leading roles. As the theatre director said when the seniors threatened revolt when the cast list for *The Wizard of Oz* was taped to the auditorium doors and Connie's name was in big, blocky letters at the top of the list, he couldn't ignore her strong—stronger, strongest—voice or the way she embodied Dorothy's vulnerability and fear as she sang "Over the Rainbow."

She made homecoming court. At lunch, she sat surrounded by cheerleaders and band nerds alike. Somehow, my sister, in her first year of high school, managed to deconstruct and reshuffle the long-standing hierarchies of the various cliques. She even bought lunch, bringing weird popularity to the greasy hamburgers and frozen pizza slices broiling under heat lamps. When she called the health teacher by his first name, it stuck, and she didn't get in a whit of trouble for it. Her glossy smile was on the front page of the monthly newsletter, an American flag ruffling in the background, her hands full of textbooks, a perfect model's smile on her face.

I watched her in the days after the cutting, wondering what signs I might have missed. Her face, at rest, had always been still and stoic, a clean, blank slate, and it remained so even though her legs were bandaged up beneath her tight jeans. She must have hurt; whispers of growled song emitted from her every now and then as the cuts reopened.

I was mostly thinking about Nicholas. We had not had sex again, and my body hummed whenever I thought of it. Something pinged and ponged inside of me, especially when he and I stood next to each other at my locker, his fingers flirting with mine, secret gestures with meanings no one else knew. When I looked at my classmates, I wondered if they were filled with this same sensation, that fluttering, intimate knowledge of another person's body. If Nicholas was hurting, he didn't show it. He smiled and whispered to me, words that left me flush, my neck tingling.

Connie's cuts healed, and the only songs of injury cropping up in our house were the usual scrapes and punctures that came with everyday living; if she had cut herself again, my sister did it somewhere no one could hear. Our dad was constantly emitting little music because he was always rifling through papers, lacerating his fingertips on printed spreadsheets and W-2s. Mom's body didn't jolt with music as often; she taught tenth- and eleventh-grade math to my friends but also liked to cook. She was smart with her knives and mostly suffered burns from spattering oil or the hot handle of a cast-iron skillet. But skin was silent; only the blood underneath, when set free, had songs to sing.

My parents made Connie go to therapy. She had to skip after-school choir, an extracurricular she thought would look good when she applied to Juilliard. She'd been using the club to practice her own song writing; I knew she was scripting a musical, and the theatre director was allowing her to borrow club time to experiment and tweak her songs. After her first therapy session, Connie barged into the house, stomping through the kitchen. She went straight to her room. I was sitting in the living room pretending to read my physics textbook, but I watched her out of the corner of my eye. Our house was an open-plan two-story, the upper floor's hall visible from the living room, a catwalk along which our bedrooms were lined up in a row, Connie's nearest the stairs and our parents' the furthest away. The bathroom where Connie had sliced herself open separated her room from mine. Climbing to the second floor, she disappeared behind the support wall that made the stairway feel like a tunnel. She reappeared in my line of vision just long enough for me to watch her slither through her door and slam it.

I turned to look at my mom, not worried about losing my place as I closed my book, having not absorbed anything I'd been reviewing about the four fundamental forces. School was almost done, Connie's first year and my last coming to a close. My mom was always tired, the brow-beating she took from my peers who didn't give a shit about geometry or trig grating on her nerves. I'd already been accepted to three colleges and had taken the scholarship money that a little liberal arts school in a sleepy northern Missouri town had offered. Nicholas was headed to UVA for tennis. We hadn't talked about what any of this would mean. I glanced up at the second floor and my sister's closed door, listening. If there was any singing to be heard, it was a tiny whisper, not enough blood to reach my ears.

‡

Nicholas and I met in study hall sophomore year. The same health teacher whom Connie would three years later call by first name, a slender man with midnight black hair and sunken eyes, had his feet up on the desk, the dry erase board behind him filled with whispers of past classes on hygiene and anaerobic exercise. Most kids didn't really study during study hall, twisting in their seats to gossip; three boys played cards at the back of the room, betting stacks of pennies and knuckle punches to the arm. I had long noticed Nicholas, who spent most of the period actually studying, glancing up at the teacher and then out the wall of windows on the far side of the room every now and then. He never looked at me. I glanced at him in profile, taking in his swoop of hair, the prominence of his Adam's apple.

The day he finally noticed me, a girl started her period midway through class, the low marine moan filling the room. Because of the acoustics, it was impossible to really tell where it was coming from. The gambling boys set down their cards and looked around, leering. Two others started laughing and scanning the girls. For a long time, nothing happened. The teacher seemed uninterested. Then, finally, a girl near the back whose name I didn't know stood and ran out without asking for a hall pass, her eyes already bleary with embarrassment as she crossed the front of the room. She was wearing a sheer blue sundress and her shoulders were piked. Laughter followed her. The echoes of her bleeding song faded beneath my classmates' horrible cackles.

The only person who seemed not to have noticed was Nicholas. He was working on math homework. His skin was browned from tennis practice. Little translucent hairs on his knuckles and forearm caught the sunlight dazzling through the windows. When he finally seemed to register the sounds around him, he looked up, straight at me, and said, "Kids are terrible," then went back to work. After the bell rang, I stopped by my locker. He appeared next to it and introduced himself, offering his hand like we were at a business meeting. I shook it. He told me his name, and I blurted out, "I know who you are."

All he did was smile, nod, and walk away. I watched him, my face bright with pleasant hurt.

‡

Connie's therapy only lasted two weeks. I don't know what she said to her psychologist to end her sessions, but after four of them she was allowed to return to after-school choir. Even though another girl in the club had passed her driver's test and offered to give Connie rides home, I stuck around after school to watch the tennis team practice. They were good, led by Nicholas in the number one singles position, and they'd amassed a quirky following of fans; several off-season athletes, including football and soccer players, milled on the bleachers outside the fenced-in courts and pretended to understand dropshots and backhands and the ideal weight distribution of first serves. A trio of art kids drew sketches, their gargantuan pads covering their thighs as they squinted into the sun to capture motion and grace. Even one goth, whose heavy pale makeup started to run if the weather was too warm, sat on the topmost row of bleachers. Like her, I sat alone, on the far edge of the first row, waiting for my sister's text telling me that choir club was over. I watched Nicholas sprint from one tram line to the other, the thwack of the ball matching the pounding rhythm of my heart. We had had sex again, and this time the only singing had been Nicholas moaning with pleasure while I gritted my teeth and tried not to come too fast.

As I watched Nicholas, I looked for signs of myself in him. I was sure that many of my classmates were having sex, but what were the markers? How might I know? With blood and its fluted songs, it was so easy to know when someone was hurt, but what about something else? Could people tell that I had changed in the last month? Or was I like Connie, the things shifting beneath my surface undetectable?

If Connie wondered why I was interested in tennis, she didn't say, just as I didn't mention her cutting. When she threw herself in my car, an old Toyota Corolla my parents had surprised me with for my eighteenth birthday, she stared out the passenger-side window, silent until we arrived at home. She emanated a vast, deep silence like a cavern so large sound couldn't travel far enough to echo.

Connie and I had never been particularly close, though we hardly hated one another. We sat in companionable quiet at dinners, and we didn't jostle with any frustrated disgust with one another in the mornings for dominion over our shared bathroom; while I brushed my teeth, I would step away from the vanity so she could comb her hair. But we'd never passed deep secrets to one another, never spent bored weekend nights in one another's rooms. She did not know about Nicholas, and I didn't know about whatever had led her to cut herself. I looked for signs of hurt or discontent as I drove, but her face was impassive as she stared out at the tree-lined streets, the public library, the punch-red brick sign at the entrance to our subdivision.

At one of the tennis team's last practices before the state championship tournament, Nicholas took a fall. He was doing a set scrimmage with the number two singles player, and they were pushing each other hard. The coach, a beefy man who pretended to teach history, stared at his players, arms crossed at his puffy chest. Near the end of a particularly long rally, the number two player hit a dropshot when Nicholas was deep in the backcourt. His shoes squealed as he rushed toward the net. Nicholas managed to scoop his racquet beneath the ball just before it hit the ground for a double bounce, but he lost his footing and tangled into and then toppled over the net.

The singing was immediate: a high-pitched squeal like a child throwing a tantrum. I, along with half of the people in the bleachers, stood immediately. Nicholas was in a heap, facing away from me, and the coach was rushing to his side. The singing continued, a meaningless warble, a cartoonish air raid siren. Everything else was silence. A hard, hot wind came whooshing across the tennis courts, rattling the batting affixed to the high fences that kept the balls from getting stuck. I felt something mush up inside me. I sat back down while the coach knelt over Nicholas, who was still tumbled on his side and gripping his knee. If he was speaking or moaning or making any noise, it was covered by the singing. Two girls near me started crying, as if they were Nicholas's best friends and were mourning his death.

Eventually, Nicholas stood, and, as if we were at an actual match, everyone started clapping. He hobbled off the court and dropped onto a bench. His eyes settled on me momentarily. The girls next to me stopped their sniffling and, instead, started humming along with the injury's singing, somehow anticipating its rhythms and dips and crests. Soon, everyone was doing the same, as though they were at a concert. Nicholas chewed a banana and blinked toward the assemblage while his coach talked to him. I was the only one doing nothing but staring, waiting and wondering if Nicholas, if Connie, if anything would be okay.

‡

The choir club held a concert at the end of the school year, the same Saturday as the state semifinals in varsity men's singles, where Nicholas was favored to win. I tried to come up with reasons not to see my sister sing, but I knew my parents would have questions. When I told him, the night before, that I couldn't go, Nicholas said it was fine. His parents were out at dinner and we were alone in his room. His fingers were splayed on my chest, tapping against my right nipple like it was a tiny snare drum. We'd gotten better at this, our bodies developing a synchronization that left us both tingling and satisfied. Nicholas was still breathing with shallow effort. We were both a little tense, his bedroom door cracked, each of us ready to spring to our boxers and khaki shorts should we hear the rumble of the garage.

"It's okay," he said. "Your family's important."

"I feel bad."

"You shouldn't." Nicholas was looking up at the popcorn ceiling, where his fan rotated slowly. His injury, like my sister's, had healed with little fanfare. There'd been no structural damage to his knee, though because the scrape was right atop his patella, it kept bursting open as he walked, its song echoing as it wept fresh blood. He had to skip practice for a few weeks because the keloid tissue was thick, blooming a grotesque snot-yellow before turning to a deep purple when it finally stopped ripping open. This had not stopped Nicholas from winning the first four rounds of singles, though he'd had to sit out the team competition and, without him, they only made the quarterfinals. If he felt any blow from that, he didn't show it.

I let out a long sigh. "I can't help how I feel."

Nicholas thumped my chest. "I know. You feel too much, I think."

I wasn't sure what to say to that. We laid in companionable silence; Nicholas liked quiet. He didn't ever feel the need to fill the silence that boomed between us.

‡

Connie's concert was held in the auditorium. The high windows that usually let in streams of light were covered in heavy black drapes so that a pair of spotlights aimed on stage burned even brighter. Instead of Connie's originals, the club sang covers of pop songs with an accompanying piano and an electric guitar whose amp had been turned down to a whisper so we could hear the singers. There were no solos, everyone's voices working together to sing the lyrics of Katy Perry, Taylor Swift, and Little Big Town. Connie stood in the back row on the mobile risers, her chin tilted up, mouth moving with crisp pronunciation. I couldn't pick her voice out from the rest. But could I see something in the way her lips rounded to cup her vowels and sustain long notes that might explain the cutting? In the flashing white of her teeth? The way her throat bobbed with vibrato? No. I neither saw nor heard anything.

Our dad insisted we stop at a frozen custard stand Connie and I loved as kids when the show was over. Connie sat next to me at a wooden picnic table and ate her vanilla custard in quiet, deliberate scoops while our parents heaped their praises upon her, telling her how proud they were. She shrugged away their congratulations.

The night was hot and muggy, mosquitoes lurking and diving to feast. I wondered how Nicholas had done in his tennis match; I thought to text him, but then my parents would ask who I was talking to. Nicholas and I had not discussed the thirteen hours' distance along I-64 that would soon ribbon between us. I think we both knew what it meant.

We finished our custard, threw away our plastic spoons on our way to the car. I felt like a human-shaped piece of flypaper. On the drive home, Dad turned on the radio to the AM station that carried Cardinals games, the announcers' voices sticky with static; the coverage dropped in and out with each pitch, creating brief flits of suspense. The bases were loaded, bottom of the eighth, the Cardinals down by two runs against the Cubs. No one in my family really cared that much about baseball, but I could tell they were all listening: Connie was boring her gaze at the radio console, as if she could will the reception into cooperation; Dad had gone silent, hands at ten and two; Mom's posture was straight and perfect as if she was in an etiquette class.

We reached our house before the inning ended. The batter had fended off a dozen pitches, fouling ball after ball into the stands. My dad let the car idle, headlights illuminating the fridge that we used for leftovers and my parents' supply of craft beer. The car grumbled but my dad made no move to cut the ignition. I thought I understood the engine, revving and waiting but with nowhere to go.

‡

Nicholas broke up with me three weeks before he left for Charlottesville. We were sitting on the end of his bed, the room hot with sunshine. He'd won the singles championship. I was able to go to his final match, where I'd sat in the stands, near the top, and clapped when everyone else clapped. I didn't call out to him or make any grand gestures when he lifted the trophy above his head.

"I just don't know how to make it work," he said, his hands in his lap.

"I know."

"I'm sorry."

I shook my head and told him not to apologize.

"I really mean it," he said.

"I know you do."

Graduation had come and gone. Tassels had been turned, caps tossed. After the ceremony, we'd gone to a party at another tennis player's house and Nicholas had been made to shotgun beers. Drunk, he'd kissed me in a corner, not seeming to worry if anyone saw. Perhaps because he was going away. Who cared what became untethered, what emerged into the light?

After we said our goodbyes, ending with an awkward hug that lasted a second too long, I walked home from his house.

A couple of kids were riding their bikes in a cul-de-sac. One of them took a turn too sharply and wobbled, then cantilevered off the side of his bike. The scrapes on his palms sung out rhythm and blues. His friend stopped and made sure he was okay. I kept walking. I didn't care about anyone else's songs.

‡

Connie cut herself again two weeks before I left for college. I was the only one to hear the singing, which growled out from the bathroom with the same volume and anger as the first time. Dad was at work, probably out on a golf course drinking lite beer with one of his clients as happened in the summer haze; Mom was in California at a conference on accelerated math courses for gifted students. I was slowly packing my things, deciding what to take with me and what to leave behind. My roommate and I had met at a Steak 'n' Shake and gone over what we might each bring. He would provide a television; I'd been given a mini-fridge as a graduation gift. I'd decided to wade through my things, donating to charity clothing I no longer wore and books I didn't read. Even some of my childhood toys that had managed to accumulate in my closet were organized into piles for giving to cousins or Goodwill.

I was folding a t-shirt when I heard the singing. My first thoughts went to Nicholas, whom I had managed to put out of mind for several weeks. Reminders of his body popped into my head from time to time, the things I liked to think I knew of him that no one else did: the way his mouth twitched when I touched the small of his back, how he liked it when I brushed his hips with my fingers when we had sex. The way his lips tightened against mine when we kissed. These reminders of what we'd been made my stomach growl, a different kind of song.

I didn't rush to Connie. I know I should have. Instead, I left my room and stood outside the bathroom door. Like last time, the singing of her blood didn't make any sense; up close, the lyrics were no more understandable than from far away. The voice was a grumble of anger and sorrow. I could feel blood beating throughout my body; my fingertips pulsed, as did my temples. My toes and crotch, too.

"Connie?"

To my surprise, the door opened. She stood before me, her right hand raised like she was taking an oath of office. A small gash smiled from her palm.

"Are you okay?" I said.

"I just needed to hear it again." She blinked, her eyes wide, pupils dilated. If I hadn't known my sister, I'd have guessed she was on drugs. But then I realized, staring at the weeping wound and listening to its song, that I didn't really know her. Not at all.

"What does it sound like?" I said.

She cocked her head, a small smile curling the edges of her lips. She'd recently cut her hair, I noticed. I wondered what else I'd missed as I prepared to leave things behind.

"I think it's beautiful." She lowered her hand, palm facing the ceiling like she was using it to catch rainfall. "Like something freshly born. Can you believe this is in me?"

"Of course I can."

She looked at me, face beatific in its relaxation. She clenched her fist, hard, so that blood pooled up around her fingertips. A little wheeze of pain slipped from her pursed lips.

"Is that why you cut yourself in the first place?" I said. "To hear what's inside you?"

"Don't we all want to know?"

I knew that couldn't be the only reason, but I didn't press. We all had things swimming in us that were for only ourselves to hear, to know. I thought of Nicholas, how his body glided across the acrylic resin of the tennis court. How his calves spasmed when we had sex. How my stomach felt when he made me orgasm.

I grabbed my sister's injured hand. She let out a soft whimper, nearly drowned out by the singing of her blood. I didn't squeeze.

Instead I let the warmth seep into my fingertips. We stood in silence, the only sound the singing, though so much else was being said without words, without language.

ACKNOWLEDGMENTS

Many thanks to the editors of the following journals for featuring these stories in their pages, sometimes in slightly altered form:

Cleaver: "Boys with Faces Like Mirrors";
Electric Spec: "Clinging";
Funicular: "Happy Birthdays";
Grist: "I Will Eat You, Drink You, I Will Be Full";
Marathon: "Forgotten Folk";
Of Rust and Glass: "Hollowed Grounds";
Rappahannock Review: "Where Can I Take You When There's
      Nowhere To Go";
Red Earth Review: "Look at Me";
The Hunger: "Heave Your Dead to the Ground";
Third Coast: "We Adore These Bodies Until They Are Gone";
Willow Review: "You Cannot Contain What's Built Up Inside";
Zone 3: "For Rent."

I am deeply indebted to my teachers, including everyone at Truman State University and the University of Louisiana. I would especially like to thank the dearly departed Marthe Reed for inviting me, before I even arrived on campus, to serve as her assistant for two years; I'm sorry I oversold how good I was at website design. My colleagues and friends at St. Charles Community College have helped create an atmosphere that has allowed me to continue my creative work, for which I cannot offer great enough thanks. Of course, all gratitude and support to my family for their continued belief in me, with the exception of that one sister. You know who you are.

ABOUT THE AUTHOR

Joe Baumann is the author of three collections of short fiction, *Sing With Me at the Edge of Paradise*, *The Plagues*, and *Hot Lips*, as well as the young adult novel, *I Know You're Out There Somewhere*. In 2019, he was a Lambda Literary Fellow in Fiction. He is the roommate of three rambunctious cats.

BOA EDITIONS, LTD.
AMERICAN READER SERIES

No. 1 *Christmas at the Four Corners of
the Earth*
Prose by Blaise Cendrars
Translated by Bertrand Mathieu

No. 2 *Pig Notes & Dumb Music: Prose on
Poetry*
By William Heyen

No. 3 *After-Images: Autobiographical
Sketches*
By W. D. Snodgrass

No. 4 *Walking Light: Memoirs and Essays on Poetry*
By Stephen Dunn

No. 5 *To Sound Like Yourself: Essays on
Poetry*
By W. D. Snodgrass

No. 6 *You Alone Are Real to Me:
Remembering Rainer Maria Rilke*
By Lou Andreas-Salomé

No. 7 *Breaking the Alabaster Jar:
Conversations with Li-Young Lee*
Edited by Earl G. Ingersoll

No. 8 *I Carry A Hammer In My Pocket
For Occasions Such As These*
By Anthony Tognazzini

No. 9 *Unlucky Lucky Days*
By Daniel Grandbois

No. 10 *Glass Grapes and Other Stories*
By Martha Ronk

No. 11 *Meat Eaters & Plant Eaters*
By Jessica Treat

No. 12 *On the Winding Stair*
By Joanna Howard

No. 13 *Cradle Book*
By Craig Morgan Teicher

No. 14 *In the Time of the Girls*
By Anne Germanacos

No. 15 *This New and Poisonous Air*
By Adam McOmber

No. 16 *To Assume a Pleasing Shape*
By Joseph Salvatore

No. 17 *The Innocent Party*
By Aimee Parkison

No. 18 *Passwords Primeval: 20 American
Poets in Their Own Words*
Interviews by Tony Leuzzi

No. 19 *The Era of Not Quite*
By Douglas Watson

No. 20 *The Winged Seed: A Remembrance*
By Li-Young Lee

No. 21 *Jewelry Box: A Collection of
Histories*
By Aurelie Sheehan

No. 22 *The Tao of Humiliation*
By Lee Upton

No. 23 *Bridge*
By Robert Thomas

No. 24 *Reptile House*
By Robin McLean

No. 25 *The Education of a Poker Player*
James McManus

No. 26 *Remarkable*
By Dinah Cox

No. 27 *Gravity Changes*
By Zach Powers

No. 28 *My House Gathers Desires*
By Adam McOmber

No. 29 *An Orchard in the Street*
By Reginald Gibbons

No. 30 *The Science of Lost Futures*
By Ryan Habermeyer

No. 31 *Permanent Exhibit*
By Matthew Vollmer

No. 32 *The Rapture Index: A Suburban
Bestiary*
By Molly Reid

No. 33 *Joytime Killbox*
By Brian Wood

No. 34 *The OK End of Funny Town*
By Mark Polanzak

No. 35 *The Complete Writings of Art Smith,
The Bird Boy of Fort Wayne, Edited
by Michael Martone*
By Michael Martone

No. 36 *Alien Stories*
By E.C. Osondu

No. 37 *Among Elms, in Ambush*
       By Bruce Weigl
No. 38 *Are We Ever Our Own*
       By Gabrielle Lucille Fuentes
No.39 *The Visibility of Things Long*
       Submerged
       By George Looney
No.40 *Where Can I Take You When There's*
       Nowhere To Go
       By Joe Baumann

COLOPHON

BOA Editions, Ltd., a not-for-profit publisher of poetry and other literary works, fosters readership and appreciation of contemporary literature. By identifying, cultivating, and publishing both new and established poets and selecting authors of unique literary talent, BOA brings high-quality literature to the public.

Support for this effort comes from the sale of its publications, grant funding, and private donations.

‡

The publication of this book is made possible, in part, by the special support of the following individuals:

Anonymous x2
Angela Bonazinga & Catherine Lewis
Christopher C. Dahl
James Long Hale
Margaret B. Heminway
Nora A. Jones
Paul LaFerriere & Dorrie Parini, *in honor of Bill Waddell*
Barbara Lovenheim
Richard Margolis & Sherry Phillips
Joe McElveney
The Mountain Family, *in support of poets & poetry*
Nocon & Associates
Boo Poulin
John H. Schultz
Robert Tortorella
Steeple-Jack Fund
William Waddell & Linda Rubel
Bruce & Jean Weigl